DEATH ON BARMOUTH BRIDGE

A NESTA GRIFFITHS MYSTERY

P. L. HANDLEY

CHAPTER 1

Nesta placed the dusty CD into the drive of her old player and closed the lid. She pressed the play button and sat back in her kitchen chair. The sound of a cheerful country and western song made her smile, and she was transported straight back to a night in Liverpool — a night almost twenty years ago.

It was hard to believe how much time had passed since Nesta and her late husband, Morgan, had visited the Edinburgh Park Dockers Club in Liverpool, where they had witnessed their first (and last) live performance from Dale Benham and his Silver Rangers. Morgan had managed to secure their tickets via an old colleague from The Wirral and could not believe that the country singer from Texas was really coming over on a UK tour (starting in a venue that he and his wife could actually drive to in less than two hours).

Nesta had originally been unfamiliar with the discography of this dashing Texan with his blue eyes and impressive side-burns, but Morgan had played his albums more than enough times around the house, until she was inevitably a convert to his catchy songs.

Dale had not let either of them down on that memorable night in Liverpool, and an ecstatic Morgan had even returned to Bala with a signed photograph of the legend himself.

Sadly, The Edinburgh Park Dockers Club was demolished many years later, but the memory of that wonderful night had stood the test of time in Nesta's head, and she would never forget the smile on her husband's face during that opening number: "Buffalos Don't Cry."

That very same song was now playing in Nesta's kitchen all those years later, and she tapped her foot beside a sleeping Jack Russell. It had been a long time since she had played her husband's CD and was pleased to hear that it was still going despite the scratches.

"Oh, Dale." Nesta looked down at the local newspaper spread out across the kitchen table. The headline was still haunting her almost as much as the music: *Country Singer Found Dead On Barmouth Bridge.*

She had not given Dale Benham much thought over the last few years, but the news of his death had come as a great shock. Not only was the singer dead at the age of sixty-three, but he had been found bludgeoned in the middle of a wooden viaduct less than thirty miles from her home.

"Life is so cruel," Nesta muttered, as she picked the newspaper back up and finished the article. The details surrounding Dale's death had been kept at a minimum, and most of the information was about the singer's long career in the world of country music. The man had never received a great deal of mainstream success but had acquired a sizable enough group of passionate fans to ensure that he could make a living playing his songs. Based out of Austin, Texas, Dale had worked hard to maintain his traditional roots, distancing himself firmly away from the more popular country music radiating out of Nashville's modern scene. He was a product of the original pioneers

— singers such as Hank Williams and Ernest Tubb — and had been determined to continue playing what *he* deemed as *"real country music"*.

Nesta nursed her morning cup of tea and tried to picture the same man she had seen lighting up the stage in his cowboy hat now lying in the middle of a footbridge. It was hard to imagine. She had not visited Barmouth since her children were young but imagined that the great viaduct hadn't changed all that much. It would take a person at least twenty minutes to cross it on foot (not that she had done) and couldn't think of a stranger place to commit a murder. The police would certainly have their work cut out for them, she thought, sipping on her *Yorkshire Tea.*

After working through all of the possible scenarios in which a person would walk that far to strike a person in the side of the head, she reached for her mobile phone and began trying to formulate a text message. There was only one other person in her life that she knew who might also find such a crime interesting, but, first, she would need to navigate her awkward keypad. Although she had grown quite competent at sending messages on her new mobile phone, it still took her at least ten minutes to write something that was legible. How on earth people managed to use both thumbs to write an entire paragraph Nesta would never know, and she had to make do with a single index finger, one letter at a time. In this message, she only needed a single sentence: *Have you seen the paper?*

She waited for the response, which eventually came in the form of another question: *Who still reads newspapers??? LOL*

Nesta sighed, and, twenty minutes later, there was a *knock* on her front door.

Darren Price entered the house with the swagger of a person who practically lived there. He was hoping that Nesta had replenished her biscuit barrel since his last visit and was craving those unusual digestives with the name that always made him chuckle.

"Fancy a *Hobnob*?" Nesta asked, as she passed her guest a cup of tea.

"I thought you'd never ask," said Darren.

It was approaching the last week of the summer holidays, and he had been bored out of his mind since returning from their memorable trip to Chester.

"How are the views going?" Nesta asked. It was not a question she would have ever thought to ask a few months ago, having never even heard of the term "streaming channel" until Darren explained it to her. Now she knew that "views" meant "subscribers" and "subscribers" meant the possibility of a new kettle. Their true crime channel had received a healthy spike of interest since their coverage of the Debbie Backes murder, and the agreement to split the royalties was paying off for both of them (Darren had even managed to buy his very own drone — a prospect that had scared the life out of Nesta).

"They're starting to plateau a bit," said Darren, munching on his biscuit. "These true crime fans are like hungry vultures. Always wanting more and more content."

"Maybe we can give them more," said Nesta with an excited grin. She slammed the newspaper down in front of him to reveal the front page.

Darren studied the headline and began reading the first paragraph. "Dale Benham? Who's he?"

Nesta was not overly surprised at the teenager's gap in knowledge. If he hadn't known who the actor Debbie Backes was, she wasn't expecting him to know a country singer (not with *his* musical tastes).

"He's got a group that plays with him called The Silver Rangers," she said.

"Never heard of him," Darren muttered. "If they're anything

like the people who played in that Honky Tonk festival you took me to, then there's a good reason."

"You mean — The Mold Rockamania?"

Darren shuddered.

"I think you'll find that Dale Benham plays in a different genre to Rockabilly," said Nesta.

"If it's not heavy metal, then it's not worth listening to." Darren stretched out his arms and continued reading the article with his cup of tea. For a split second, he resembled an older man, enjoying his morning newspaper with a nice hot brew.

Nesta resisted the urge to pour the drink over his stubborn little head and tried to steer their conversation to the recent crime. "Anyway," she said, "Dale has a big following. They say that he was in Barmouth to attend a country and western festival. He was staying at a guesthouse in the town."

"I thought you said he had a big following?" Darren asked. "Why would a country western star be playing a festival in *Barmouth*? It's hardly Nashville."

Nesta frowned. "I think you'll find Barmouth is lovely this time of year, actually — and busy. Besides, this is the first leg of a UK tour."

Darren still wasn't convinced and continued scanning the article. "How long is this bridge?"

"Are you telling me that you've never been to Barmouth?" Nesta stared at him in disbelief. This young man never ceased to amaze her. "And you live in Bala?"

"I've never been to Llandrillo, either. And that's only down the road." Darren shrugged. "So, what? I doubt that I'm missing out."

Nesta folded up her arms in a sulk. Her plan to excite the teenager over this new case was not going well, and she was going to have to try harder. "I was thinking we could scope this whole thing out. Maybe see if we can get some rooms in that guesthouse Dale was staying in. Retrace his steps?"

Darren scoffed. "Yeah, right. The last time I agreed to a room to stay in, we ended up in the same one — with me on the sofa!"

"I doubt that a Barmouth guesthouse will be as expensive as *The Legion Hotel* in Chester!"

The teenager shook his head. "I'm not spending the last week of my summer holidays in Barmouth, covering a bloke that none of our viewers have ever heard of. It's not worth it!" He flipped over the newspaper in search of the sudoku puzzle.

Nesta was about to give up, when a sudden thought popped into her head. She let out a mischievous smile and sat down opposite him. "You know that Barmouth Bridge is over half a mile long?"

Darren didn't even take his eyes off the newspaper. "Is it? That's nice."

"Probably one of the longest viaducts in the country." Nesta leant forward as though she was a crocodile trying to seduce a buffalo into having a nice, cold drink. "It crosses a giant estuary, and you can walk the entire thing. The view is absolutely stunning. I can only imagine what it must look like from above."

Darren's eyes slowly looked up. "*Above*?"

"I'm sure it would be an epic view. I bet a shot like that alone would get lots of views." Nesta sighed and nursed her mug of tea. "Course, you would need a way to get that high up in the first place. Not that I know about these things. All very technical. You'd probably need a crane or a helicopter... or something else that can fly up really high. Something like a —"

"Drone?" Darren's eyes were wide with excitement.

Nesta clicked her fingers. "Yes, that would do the trick. A drone would work." She blew on her hot drink and could practically hear the teenager's mind whirling around with ideas. Her mouth twisted itself into a smug grin.

CHAPTER 2

Nesta had opted for a slightly different route to Barmouth than the one Darren's phone was recommending. Once they had passed the town of Dolgellau, she took a turn towards a place called Penmaenpool.

"Where are you going?" Darren asked, staring down at the device on his lap.

"I'm taking us the fun way," said Nesta.

"The only fun way is the *quickest* way."

Nesta rolled her eyes. "Why you insist on having that sat-nav thing on anyway is beyond me. I know my way to Barmouth."

"I like to see how far we've got left to go."

His driver groaned. "How about you look around and enjoy the journey? You'll know when we're almost there when you see the sea. You don't need a phone to tell you that — just your eyes."

Darren ignored her advice and continued to stare at the blue line snaking across the screen. Twenty-five minutes to go, the remaining journey counter said. The teenager sighed and listened to the sound of Dale Benham's voice humming out through the speakers. The singer's *Greatest Hits* album was already on its second pass since leaving Bala, and the songs were starting to grow on him (as hard as it was to admit).

"You see," said Nesta, catching sight of his toe tapping. "I told you Dale's got some good ones."

"It's alright, I suppose. He's better than I thought he'd be for a country singer. It's usually all yodelling and steel guitars."

"I don't know what country music *you've* been listening to, but Dale was as edgy as any of your metal-head bands. Where do you think their style came from in the first place? Country, rock, blues... the roots are all intertwined."

"I didn't ask for a music lesson," Darren muttered. "I'm just saying the lyrics aren't bad, that's all."

"Well," said Nesta. "I wasn't asking for a critical review, either. You can take Dale Benham or leave him."

Darren was about to pull his hat down for a quick snooze, when he saw that they were approaching a gatehouse with a wooden toll bridge on the other side.

"Where are we going now?" he asked.

Nesta wound her window down and grabbed her purse. "I haven't crossed this bridge in years. The children used to love it." She smiled at the man approaching her window. "Two and a half, please!" Her joke had not landed as well as intended, and the man gazed over at the grumpy looking teenager with a Jack Russell at his feet.

"That'll be a pound."

Nesta tried to hide her horror and handed over her fare. "That's gone up a bit. It was twenty pence when I last came."

The Citroën began rolling across the bridge at a speed so slow that Darren was beginning to suspect that there was something wrong with the engine. This rickety, bumpy ride did not feel like a short cut, and he prayed that they would make it to the other side of the estuary without it collapsing.

"Well," said Nesta, once they were finally back on a main road. "That was fun, wasn't it?"

Darren turned to look at her as though she had lost her mind. "Oh, yeah. Worth every penny of that pound."

Ten minutes later, and they could finally see the sea through their front windscreen, as the road curved up and down beside the Mawddach Estuary. They came down into Barmouth as the train was crossing the great bridge, and Darren watched the line of carriages disappear into the distance.

"It's big alright," he said.

His driver nodded and drove them up a road so steep that it reminded the teenager of a rollercoaster. The only problem with *this* rollercoaster was that its driver didn't appear all that confident, as they continued onwards and upwards into the hills.

"The guy didn't pick a spot in town?" Darren asked, sinking back into his chair from the force of sheer gravity. Even Hari was struggling to stay still whilst sliding backwards in the footwell.

"This is technically still in town," said Nesta, reaching for her map. "Just the higher-up part. I believe they call it Old Barmouth. He must have been craving a good view."

Darren saw her trying to shake out the map and snatched it away. "Leave the map to me. You just concentrate on the road." The teenager began scratching his head, having forgotten that everything on a map appeared to be flat.

After several arguments about the correct route for their last leg of the journey, these two out-of-towners eventually came across a large building overlooking a steep cliff edge. The large guesthouse was made from the same grey stone as all of the other surrounding properties, only this building looked a lot more worse for wear. Bryn Lodge, as it was officially called, felt as though it had been carved out of solid rock and looked down upon Barmouth like a bruised eye.

"I've never seen the town from *this* angle before," said Nesta, stepping out of her car and walking across the muddy drive. She took a deep breath of salty air. "I feel like a seagull from up here."

"Don't talk to me about seagulls," Darren muttered. "The last time I saw one of those, a group of them stole my burger on a school trip."

Nesta smiled. "I'd say you're safe up here."

"Am I?" The teenager turned around to look at their new accommodation. "The last person who stayed here got murdered in the middle of the night. Plus, the *Addams Family* have better standards than this place."

Trust him to ruin a nice moment, Nesta thought, and headed to the boot for their luggage. "Cheer up," she said. "You're on holiday now."

Darren had his own ideas of a holiday, and they did *not* include sunburn and a stick of rock.

"Mrs Griffiths?"

Anwen Neville headed down a flight of stone steps to greet her guests. The woman in her sixties still had her cooking apron on and possessed the largest pair of glasses Darren had ever seen.

"Yes," said Nesta, reaching out for a handshake. "You can call me Nesta."

Her host grinned with a thick layer of lipstick. "Then you can call me Anwen. Welcome to Barmouth!" She turned to look at Darren. "I can see you've brought your grandson."

The teenager waited for the woman to be corrected, but Nesta couldn't be bothered to explain.

"It's a lovely property you have here," Nesta said, taking another look at the view.

Anwen nodded. "Yes, we're very lucky. I love seeing our guests arriving for the first time. It's a busy time of year, but I wouldn't have it any other way."

"How many rooms do you have?" Darren asked with a suspicious frown. After his last experience staying somewhere with Nesta, he was determined not to be fooled again.

"We have four rooms altogether," said Anwen. "My husband and I live in the house across the road, so we can easily pop in and out."

"And how many rooms do *we* have booked?"

Anwen chuckled and ruffled the teenager's hair. "He's a curious little thing, isn't he?" She glanced down at his *Deathdemons* t-shirt with great disapproval. "I hope you're well-behaved for your grandma. You remind me of my son. He was a very naughty boy when he was your age."

Darren felt his blood boil. "Actually —"

"Don't worry," said Nesta. "We'll be no trouble."

Anwen gave the furious teenager a long stare before pulling out a *Milky Way* bar from her pocket and handing it to him. "There's a good lad. Here — a little welcoming present from your Auntie Anwen."

The teenager was about to snap at her, until he realised how hungry he was and took the chocolate bar with a shrug.

"Right," said Anwen, pointing to the luggage in the open boot. "Why don't you help your dear nana and bring in the bags for her? I can't wait to give you the full tour!"

The inside of Anwen's guesthouse turned out to be a complete contrast to its dark exterior. The pink walls were enough to disturb Darren from the moment they entered through the front door, and the furniture and carpets hadn't appeared to have changed in many decades.

"Are you sure this isn't an old people's home?" Darren whispered into Nesta's ear, as they stood in the living room area.

Nesta hushed him and continued to give Anwen a polite nod, as she pretended to listen.

"All of our guests can make themselves at home in our

communal dining and living room areas." She pointed to an old television in the corner. "We don't have any of those fancy channels with all the films —"

"Like *Netflix*?" Darren asked.

Anwen coughed. "Yes, that's right. We don't have anything like that. But there's at least five channels on there. Which is enough for anyone in my opinion."

The disappointed teenager folded up his arms in a sulk.

Nesta was more interested in the framed photograph over on the mantlepiece. "Is that who I think it is?" She walked over to the small fireplace and saw an image of Dale Benham standing outside the same property they were staying in. Anwen was right beside him, and his signature was scribbled over the top.

The host clutched her hands with delight. "You're a Dale Benham fan?"

"Well," said Nesta. "I'd say *fan* is a strong word. My husband certainly was, and we have his records in the house. I was shocked to hear the news."

Anwen nodded. "We're still very much in mourning here. It's all so fresh. You see —" She looked around the room and acted as though she was about to share a secret. "I'm not really supposed to tell you this — my husband would go mad — but Dale was a guest of ours on the night that he died."

Nesta cupped her mouth. "No! Surely not."

Darren shook his head in reaction to her poor acting skills. "

"Yes," said Anwen, acting like she had been dying to tell someone. "He was staying at this very house. In fact, I was one of the last people to see him alive."

"Really?" Nesta asked. "How shocking!"

Anwen stood beside her, and they both gazed down at the photograph. "This was actually taken on his last trip."

"*Last* trip?" Nesta popped on her glasses to get a better look. "You mean, Dale has been to Barmouth before?"

"Many times, actually. He has relatives who live here. Whenever he's done a UK tour, Barmouth has always been included as one of the stops." She began stroking the glass inside the picture frame. "I was already a fan. When I first met him after one of his gigs, I told him he was always welcome to stay at my local guesthouse — free of charge. The next year, he took me up on it."

Nesta nodded. "Why wouldn't you? Free room and board would have been very enticing."

"He loved my fry-ups," said Anwen, seemingly wiping a tear from her eye. "Anyway, let's show you the rooms."

Darren waited for the woman to disappear through the doorway before grabbing Nesta by the arm. "Surely you don't still want to stay here with *that* woman around," he whispered.

"I don't know what you mean," said Nesta.

"Oh, come on! That woman's clearly a raving lunatic. We probably won't last the night!"

"Don't be so silly," Nesta snapped. "You watch far too many —"

"What? True crime channels on the internet? Like the one we do?" He could sense her cynicism.

"I was *going* to say — Alfred Hitchcock films..."

"Alfred Hitch — what?" Darren shook his head and pulled out his phone. "I'm going to be recording every minute I can in case it's the last case we ever cover. It'll be like *The Blair Witch Project* — only with a scarier witch!"

Nesta hushed him. "She seems perfectly friendly."

"Are you both coming?" Anwen called out from the top of the stairs.

Darren smiled. "After you, then."

The second floor had the same coat of pink as the first and had a narrow hallway with a series of doors on one side and a single window on the other. There was a stale odour in the air that made the two guests shudder, and Nesta was surprised by the cool temperature, considering the warmth outside.

"There's a bathroom at the very end," said Anwen. "We only have one other guest in at the moment, so there shouldn't be too much of a queue in the morning."

"We're all sharing the same bathroom?" asked Darren.

Nesta gave him a nudge and noticed that one of the doors was open. She peered inside, as they went past and saw an acoustic guitar propped up against the wall. "Was that the room?"

Anwen turned around to see what she was looking at. "Oh," she said, coming back to close the door. "Yes, that was Dale's room. I can't even bring myself to move anything. The police have finished their inspections, but I need to sort out what happens to his belongings." She smiled. "I thought about the idea of making the whole room a shrine. Maybe open it up to the public. But my husband is adamant we need it for new guests." Anwen opened up the two doors on the very end of the hallway. "Anyway, these are your rooms over here."

Darren let out a sigh of relief at the sight of two rooms.

"I think you'll find that they have everything you need," Anwen continued. "But holler if you need anything."

Nesta was more preoccupied with Dale Benham's room, and she looked back at the closed door. The thought of what clues might be lurked inside was too overwhelming. For now, she would have to be patient.

CHAPTER 3

"I'm telling you," said Darren. "That woman's a psychopath."

Nesta continued unpacking her suitcase and shook her head. "She seems perfectly nice to me."

"Are you kidding? Even Hari doesn't like her." He pointed to the snoozing Jack Russell on Nesta's bed. "I wouldn't be surprised if she's the one who killed off that country singer. I bet you she wanted to stuff him for that shrine of hers."

"Keep your voice down," Nesta snapped.

The teenager began comparing her room to his own and was adamant that it was in much better condition (which wasn't saying very much in *this* guesthouse). "Oh, I can guarantee she's listening. Probably got some peep holes or secret cameras everywhere. She gives me the creeps." He peered out of the window and could see the town of Barmouth down below. "I just don't get why a famous country singer would choose to stay in a dump like this? His career must have been *really* down the toilet."

"It was certainly very cheap," said Nesta. "That's why I booked you a separate room."

"Wow, thanks." Darren looked up at the mould across the

edges of the ceiling. "She said he was staying here for free. I'm beginning to wonder if he was actually a prisoner."

"You're letting your imagination get the better of you." Nesta sat down on the edge of her bed and heard a loud *crack*. "We can't go jumping to conclusions already. How about you fetch that last bag and take a moment to clear your head? The sea air will do you good."

Darren sighed and grabbed the lead. "Fine, but I'm taking Hari in case anything happens to me."

Nesta rolled her eyes and watched them both head back out into the hallway.

As Darren and his furry bodyguard reached the bottom of the stairs, they were faced with a scowling Anwen.

"And where do you think you're going?" she asked.

The teenager was surprised by her sudden change in tone. She had transformed from a cheerful host to someone with an enormous bee in her bonnet. "Uh, I'm heading out to the car. It's a free country, isn't it?"

"Don't you take that dreadful attitude with me," Anwen hissed. "I've got my eye on you, young man. I know your sort. And I won't be standing for any of it under my roof."

"I don't know what you mean," said Darren.

Anwen glared at him. "What were you filming earlier?"

"Filming?"

"You had your phone out during the tour. Don't think I'm stupid. I know what those devices are capable of with their apps and AI..."

Darren almost choked on his laugh. "That's not how AI works."

The woman continued to peer inside the depths of his soul, and it made him very nervous. She reminded him of a teacher, but at least Mrs Kirby from Geography wasn't capable of smothering him in his sleep. "What I mean is," he added, "I was just taking pictures to show my mam when I get home."

Anwen let out a dissatisfied grunt and pointed her finger at him. "Like I said — I'm watching you. There will be no trouble in this house." She heard the Jack Russell begin to growl, as she stepped into the teenager's personal space. The woman took a step back and continued up the stairs, leaving a disturbed Darren to continue his journey to the car.

Outside, he could finally breathe some fresh air. The sound of seagulls reminded him of where he was, and he was beginning to think this whole trip was a bad idea. Drone shot or no drone shot — he might as well have been staying in a haunted house with a Transylvanian Count.

"Hey, there, fella!"

Darren turned to see a man with an enormous beard and a cowboy hat on his head. This scruffy individual had a shirt that was far too small for his large stomach, and the buttons looked as though they were going to burst off at any moment. It turned out that the Irishman was in fact talking to the Jack Russell and hurried over to stroke him on the head.

"He yours?" the man asked.

"He belongs to my friend," said Darren.

"I used to have one just like him back in Tennessee." He stood up and offered out his hand. "Nick Franklin! Pleased to meet you." Nick paused with a grin. "Ah! *There's* the look. I thought you recognised me."

A confused Darren stared at him. "Have we met?"

Nick howled with laughter and slapped him on the back. "That's a good one! *Have we met?!*" He gave the young man a moment and raised up his arms. "Nick Franklin? Country prince of the North West? Former *Midwestern Hillbilly Strummer Of The Year* winner 2011? No?" He pulled out his vape and began puffing away. "Okay, maybe before your time. Don't feel bad. You kids are all confused these days. I don't blame you."

"Midwestern?" Darren asked. "Does that mean you're from America? You sound Irish."

Nick nodded. "Your ears are spot on. Originally from County Cork — moved to Austin, Texas as a younger man. Now residing in Stoke-on-Trent. Hence why they call me the country prince of the North West."

"Wow, you get around." Darren grabbed the last remaining bag from the car and looked down at the man's cowboy boots. He had always wanted to visit the United States, ever since his grandparents had brought him back a *Hard Rock Café* t-shirt from Orlando, Florida. They were the only people he had ever met to cross the Atlantic and had spent hours showing him their holiday snaps, which included a visit to *Universal Studios*. "What's Texas like?"

Nick sat himself down against the edge of the boot before Darren could close it and caused the entire car to dip slightly from the added weight. "Ah, The Lone Star State. I place her very dear to my heart. You like steak?"

"Who doesn't?" asked Darren.

"Then you'd love it." He puffed out another cloud of vapor. "You ever hear of the seventy-two-ounce steak challenge?" Darren shook his head. "There's this steak house in Amarillo. If you can eat the entire seventy-two-ounce steak in one sitting, then you win the challenge."

The teenager was already fascinated. "What do you win?"

"You get the entire meal free of charge." Nick patted his bulging stomach. "Only ten percent of challengers have ever succeeded — and I'm one of them!"

"Wow," said Darren, genuinely impressed.

"Yep," said Nick, raising his chin up, proudly. "I miss Texas. It made me into the country singer I am today."

Darren had a sudden thought. "Isn't that where Dale Benham was from?"

The mere mention of the country singer's name caused Nick to remove his hat. "You've heard of Dale Benham?" he asked, slightly annoyed. He couldn't believe that the young man knew the name of Dale Benham but not Nick Franklin (the country and western prince of the English North West).

"He was staying here, wasn't he?"

Nick nodded, gravely. "Dale was a former mentor of mine. When I found out that he was down here for the annual *Barmouth Country And Western Festival* this year, I couldn't believe it. Luckily, I managed to book myself a last-minute slot and dropped him a line. Dale even suggested a cheap place for me to stay. We hadn't seen each other in years."

"What do you mean he was a mentor?" Darren asked.

"He taught me everything I know about the business," said Nick. "When I met Dale, I was just an amateur trying to break into the music industry. He taught me how to be a professional — literally. He said that you should never judge yourself until you've done a hundred gigs. And he was right. The guy really took me under his wing, and I followed him around the midwest. He played everywhere: dive bars, festivals, diners — you name it. That's when I learnt what a *real* musician did. It was all just hard grafting just like any other trade." Nick let out a proud smile. "When I first met Dale, I'd written some songs, and he had a look at them for me. He said I had a natural talent for it. They were fun times." Nick saw that the teenager was listening intently to every word. "Do you play any instruments yourself?"

Darren nodded. "Sort of. I'm learning the guitar at the moment."

"Why, that's great!" The musician clapped his hands. "You won't regret it. There's something about playing an instrument that makes you feel alive. It's a very special relationship. You can play for years and still discover new things. Who's your teacher?"

"Oh, I just teach myself. I've got this online app that shows me how to play the chords."

Nick tried not to laugh. "An *app*? You're trying to learn the guitar with a *phone app*?"

The teenager could sense the judgement and frowned. "I've only just started, like."

The man slapped him on the back and chuckled. "Well, good luck. But if you need a few pointers, feel free to give me a shout whilst you're here. I like to give back, you know? Someone did the same for me when I was younger." He lifted up a guitar case and stretched out his arm. "Now, if you don't mind, I'm going to rest my eyes for a while. I'll see you around."

Darren nodded and watched the bearded man stroll off, merrily, back into the building. For a man who had recently lost a good friend, his mood seemed very cheerful.

CHAPTER 4

Nesta closed the bathroom door behind her and peered down the empty hallway. The closed door at the far end was drawing her in as though it were whispering. The mysteries of Dale Benham's room were still playing on her mind, and she couldn't help but take the opportunity for a quick peek.

Fortunately, the rooms at Bryn Lodge didn't seem to have locks on the doors, a fact that had highly disturbed her fellow lodger. Darren hated the idea that a person could simply just walk into his room in the middle of the night, and Nesta had reassured him that he had nothing to worry about. After all, this was a guesthouse in Barmouth we were talking about — not a motel with Norman Bates in charge.

The door to Dale's room creaked as it opened, and Nesta had just managed to catch a brief glimpse inside, when she sensed a presence behind her.

"I think you might have the wrong room."

She turned around to see a suspicious Anwen Neville, who was clutching a mug of hot tea.

"Oh," said Nesta, stepping back to get a good look at the

doorway. "Is this not my room? How silly of me!" She began counting the doors and nodding. "That's right. Mine's that one over there."

Anwen stared at her. "Easy mistake to make." She reached over and closed Dale's door. "Can I offer you a cuppa?"

The two women were soon standing in the downstairs kitchen, whilst the kettle seemed to take forever to boil. Nesta began inspecting the row of framed photographs on the wall and realised that Anwen was featured in every single one.

"I see you've met a lot of interesting people," she said, gazing at some of the smiling faces. Each photograph had Anwen standing, gleefully, beside a famous musician, and an autograph was displayed in every corner. Nesta's eyes were drawn to one of these individuals in particular, a man with a white cowboy hat and a shirt with a floral pattern covering the chest and shoulders: Dale Benham.

Anwen stood beside her and admired her collection. It gave her immense pleasure, and she beamed with pride whilst working through them. "That's Bucky Reynolds, and there's Mimi Don, Carl Springs..." There was a short pause, as she reached the photograph of Dale Benham. "And, of course, the legend himself."

"It sounds like you really were a big fan of his," said Nesta.

"I adored him," said Anwen. "I bought all of his records. I even made special trips to Texas to attend his gigs. There was no singer quite like Dale."

"My husband was a big fan, too. He introduced me to his music."

Anwen turned to her with a smile. "Your husband sounds like he had good taste." Her face suddenly went sour. "I wish mine was not so close-minded."

"He doesn't like Dale?"

Her host scoffed. "He can't stand the whole genre. As for

Dale, well, I think he was just jealous. Anyone would be when it comes to a man like that."

Nesta turned her attention to a man standing in the doorway. Richard Neville had a frown that would curdle a glass of milk and a grey moustache that covered up his top lip.

Anwen had not noticed her husband until now, but she didn't seem fazed.

"Aren't you supposed to be at your appointment?" Richard asked.

His wife rolled her eyes and threw out the last of her tea. "Since when were you my timekeeper? It's not like you're early for anything." She turned to Nesta with an apologetic sigh. "Sorry, must dash. I've got a doctor's appointment. That's the first time he's ever cared about my health."

Richard shook his head, as his wife marched out of the room. "I do apologise if she's bored you with the usual stories."

Nesta saw that he was looking at the signed photographs. "Oh, not at all. I'm something of a country fan myself."

The man let out a grunt and went to grab himself a drink of water. "You two should get on like a house on fire, then. Personally, I don't get any of it."

"You mean, music in general?"

"The country western genre, the cowboy look, the songs about places I've never even been to or care about." Richard took a gulp of water. "Why should I care about some moon in Kentucky? I live in Barmouth."

"Well," said Nesta, sensing that the man felt quite strongly about the subject. "Barmouth is host to an annual country and western festival."

Richard groaned. "Don't remind me. It's my worst time of year — visitors walking around town like they're John Wayne. Get a *real* hobby."

"And what exactly would you class as a real hobby, Mr

Neville?" Nesta folded up her arms and waited for a worthy response.

"Fly fishing," said Richard without even hesitating. "Or any sort of fishing in general. Not that I get much time to do that."

"I imagine this place must keep you busy," said Nesta.

The man stared at her as though she were bonkers. "*This* place? You think we make enough money from people staying here?" He let out a laugh and remembered that he was speaking with a paying customer. "What I mean is — our little B&B is very popular, obviously, but Anwen and I both have full-time day jobs." He paused and let out a sigh. "Not that I would class my wife's job as full time."

Nesta gave him a cynical nod. "What exactly do you do for a living, Mr Neville, if you don't mind me asking?"

"I'm a physics teacher."

"Are you really?" Nesta couldn't help but smile. "Every physics teacher she had ever known had been exactly alike: practical, sensible and very grounded (perhaps with the help of studying all that gravity). "How interesting."

"I think it is," said Richard. "Although, the students could certainly take a lot more interest than they do."

"Oh, I feel your pain." Nesta was still smiling. "I was a teacher myself. You should try keeping the attention of a load of hormonal teenagers when you're in the middle of a Shakespearean sonnet."

Richard's shoulders lowered, and he already appeared to be more relaxed now that he knew he was talking to a fellow educator. "This business was supposed to be my fast-track into retirement." He looked up at the mouldy ceiling. "So far, it's turning into a money pit from hell. It was a real fixer-upper when we bought it. Only we've barely managed to fix anything. The roof needs doing, we have rising damp, the boiler's on the blink..."

Nesta listened and tried to hide her concern. If this is how

Richard Neville *normally* spoke to his guests, it was no wonder the business was struggling. "It sounds very stressful."

"You can say that again," said Richard, crossing his arms. "And now I'm spending my summer holidays trying to keep it running."

"What does your wife teach?" Nesta asked. "You said that she is a teacher as well?"

The man's mood worsened. He looked over his shoulder to make sure it was safe. "*Teacher* is a strong word. She gives piano lessons. And sometimes the harp. But those have started to decline in recent years. My wife has very little patience with young people. And I have no patience at all. But at least my lessons are mandatory."

"She mentioned you have a son?"

Richard nodded. "I wouldn't say that he's *young* anymore. Kris is a grown man now — not that he acts like it!"

Nesta wandered over to the wall of fame and began studying the photograph of Dale Benham. "I imagine having a celebrity like Dale staying here would have been good publicity."

"Don't get me started on that man," said Richard, joining her at the photographs. "I hate to speak ill of the dead, but he caused me nothing but trouble."

"What kind of trouble?" asked Nesta.

"He was staying here Scott free for a start!" Richard snarled his lip. "Anwen was insistent that he didn't need to pay a penny. And, boy, did he take advantage — the washed-up has-been." The man huffed. "Actually, I take that back. You can't be a has-been if you never *were* a thing in the first place."

"He must have been well-known enough for my husband to be a fan," said Nesta. "Morgan was hardly one to seek out obscure artists."

Richard shrugged. "He may have acquired a decent enough following back in his day, at least in the country western scene.

But he's practically unheard of in this country. Most people I know have never heard of him."

"Your wife was certainly a fan."

"And don't we all know it! I was sick of hearing about the man *before* he turned up in my guesthouse. She cost us a fortune in concert tickets and flights to America. Why couldn't she have fallen in love with someone local? Like Dafydd Iwan?"

Nesta was struck by the word "love" and wondered how much of Richard's disdain was caused by jealousy. "What was Dale like? As a person, I mean. Was he a difficult guest?"

Richard took a moment to picture that smarmy man, strolling around his property like he owned it. "All guests are difficult. But Dale was just a freeloading leech. He must have been really struggling financially to stay here as much as he did." A sly grin crept over his face. "I cornered him, once. Told him that he needed to pay his way. I said he could take advantage of my wife, but I was a whole different kettle of fish. He didn't like that. But I still didn't get any money out of him. The tight-fisted sponger. Despite his living conditions, he really thought he was Johnny Cash. He'd walk around Barmouth like the Pope — him and his entourage of muppets."

"You mean, his band?" Nesta thought about Dale's backing group — The Silver Rangers. They were not as well-known as their frontman, but Dale was rarely seen without them. "Where do they stay?"

"I hear they're big campers," said Richard with a shudder. "They look like a bunch of ageing hippy travellers. It's quite sad, I suppose. If Dale Benham's career was so tragic by the end, I can't imagine what it was like for *them*. Anwen says they hire a couple of campervans and park up outside *The Craig Tavern* on the edge of town. The landlord is apparently a fan and lets them use his field. Free-of-charge, probably — another sucker!"

"And they've never stayed here?" asked Nesta.

Richard shook his head. "I'd never allow that rabble in this place. Dale was bad enough, and I had to draw the line. It shows the type of leader he was to let his band sleep rough whilst he had a roof over his head." He looked back up at the ceiling. "Or *just about* over his head."

Nesta finished the rest of her tea and headed back to her room. After listening to her host's second rant about the state of his property, she couldn't wait to start enjoying the facilities. Bryn Lodge certainly had its fair share of problems, and Nesta suspected that she had barely scratched the surface.

CHAPTER 5

Nesta spread out her map across the bed. She placed her finger in the middle of Barmouth Bridge and scribbled a large dot. "Please don't get that thing out in here," she said.

Darren was kneeling on the floor, tinkering with his drone. "I'm not going to fly it indoors," he said. "I'm not *that* stupid."

Nesta stared down at the spiderlike contraption as though it was a wild animal about to pounce. Hari was also cautious and remained poised under the bed, growling.

"What's the matter with him?" Darren asked. He grabbed his user manual and began searching for remote batteries.

"He doesn't like the drone," said Nesta. "And I don't blame him."

Darren studied his instructions like a child on Christmas morning. "You know this has up to a ten-kilometre range?"

"I speak Welsh, English and a little bit of French. But the language you've just uttered is lost on me."

The teenager sighed. "It means that we could see every corner of Barmouth and not even have to go outside." He lifted up a small monitor. "We can watch the drone's entire journey from the comfort of our room. How cool is that?"

Now it was Nesta's turn to sigh. "Next you'll be telling me we can just order our food and have it brought to our door."

"Uh, yeah. People have been able to do that for ages."

Nesta climbed to her feet and began circling the room. "I mean, why bother going anywhere at all? We can just stay in bed all day and do nothing."

Darren lifted up his screwdriver. "Sounds good to me."

"There's a whole world out there." Nesta approached the windowsill and gazed out at the town down below. "But let's just experience everything on a screen the size of a ciabatta roll." She knew her words were not being heard and began rooting through the selection of tourist guides piled up on the coffee table. A pamphlet caught her eye, and she saw the heading: *Barmouth Country And Western Festival Guide*. There was still another week left, and it was decided that the schedule might come in handy for later.

"Where are all the power sockets?" Darren asked, looking around the room. "It's like living in the dark ages staying at this place. They don't even have wifi."

Nesta headed back to the comfort of her bed and pointed at the drone. "You're not plugging that thing in my room."

"I'm only charging up the battery!"

"Well, you can do it in your own room." Nesta lay back against her pillow. "I'm not being woken up in the middle of the night by some flashing UFO." She pondered for a moment and grabbed her map.

Darren saw the intensity in her face. "What is it?" He let out a smile. "Don't tell me that you think a UFO killed Dale Benham."

"Don't be silly," said Nesta. "The last UFO sighting around

these parts was by a farmer in Llangower." Darren stared at her. "I'm serious! Gwyn Thomas went on an *S4C* programme and everything. He saw one near his farm. Anyway, I was just thinking about Dale's journey across the bridge…" She opened up her map again, and Darren joined her on the bed. Nesta ran her finger across a long line that made its way across the estuary of the River Mawddach. "We know that his body was found about halfway across the bridge, but we don't know what direction he was heading in."

"Does it matter?" Darren asked, as he watched her rotating the map. "Either way, he didn't make it all the way across."

"No," said Nesta, "but it matters which direction the killer was heading from." She pointed to the area of land on the other side of the estuary. "I assume that Dale or his killer had walked from the direction of town. But what if one of them had come from the other side? That opens up a whole host of possibilities."

"Correct me if I'm wrong," said Darren. "But isn't that a bad thing? The last thing we need is a load of new scenarios and suspects."

Nesta frowned and almost slapped the top of his head with the map. "Trust you to turn a positive into a negative."

"You sound like my physics teacher."

Nesta grabbed her notebook and began scribbling. "Speaking of physics teacher…"

"What's that for?" asked Darren, pointing at the notebook. "I've never seen you write anything down before."

"I've decided that we need to be more organised with these investigations. Any detective worth their salt carries a notebook."

"Is that what we are now? *Detectives?*"

"To be honest," said Nesta, sitting up to think about it, "I don't know *what* we are. But you might find it useful to take notes."

Darren groaned. "Now you *really* sound like my teacher. There's no way I'm having to write stuff as well. I make videos — not essays. I'm just here to shoot."

Nesta shook her head and turned back to the map. "Well, it's a good job *one* of us is organised. Or we wouldn't get anywhere." She readjusted her glasses and followed the bridge all the way to town. "Now, first thing's first. We need to work out why Dale was crossing that bridge in the first place. *Someone* must have seen him. There *has* to be a witness."

"When did Mrs What's-Her-Name last see him?" Darren asked with a disgruntled frown. "I bet she's got no alibi for that night."

"That's actually not a bad idea." Nesta began scribbling in her notebook. "We can ask her at breakfast."

The teenager shuddered. "I'm not eating the breakfast at this place. Or I might not make it to the bridge at all tomorrow."

"Don't be silly," said Nesta. "Most poisons can take at least a few hours to pass through the system — the more practical ones, anyway. I doubt Anwen would want you keeling over in her dining room."

"Thanks," Darren muttered. "That's very reassuring."

Nesta looked up at the clock. "Dale's body was found in the morning, according to the news report. If we can find out what time he was last seen, that should narrow down the window of time in which he was killed."

"I don't see how the time of death helps us," said Darren. "Even if we knew for sure that he was killed at midnight, that doesn't get us any closer. Everyone would say that they were in bed."

Nesta sighed. "We have to start somewhere. Determining the time of death is standard police procedure. These investigations have a system."

"If these systems work so well," said Darren, "then we can

just wait for the police to find the killer. But something tells me they won't have a clue on this one." He climbed off the bed and returned to tending to his precious drone. "I say stick with the process I've always used to find something; it's worked alright for me in the past."

"And what intricate process is that, exactly?"

Darren gave her question some thought and realised it was a good one. "I call it *Price's Law*. We stab around in the dark until we hit something. The quicker and harder we stab, the quicker we'll find what we're looking for. The knife's a metaphor, obviously. Unless you think we need one."

Nesta listened with that concerned look on her face. This was all going to take a lot longer than she had anticipated.

CHAPTER 6

The breakfast at Bryn Lodge was nothing to write home about (not that Nesta and Darren were expecting much). The cooked breakfast was suspiciously rubbery and had likely been re-heated from the previous day. Even the milk was slightly off — literally — and the two guests were beginning to suspect that the most "important meal of the day" was also going to be their last in quite some time (depending on how thoroughly the bacon was cooked).

"Any more tea?"

Anwen had appeared at the table with a teapot in her hand, and Nesta would not have been surprised if it contained a single teabag that had been reused to the point of being tasteless.

"I'm quite alright," she said. "Thank you."

"And how about you?" Anwen asked, turning to the teenager with a harsh scowl.

Darren took a gulp of his orange juice and shook his head.

"It must get quite busy in here when you've got a full house," said Nesta, gazing around at the cramped dining room. There were only two other tables, which had been unnaturally forced into the small space, and it was already a tight squeeze with just the two of them.

"Oh, yes." Anwen stood tall in her cooking apron covered in cowboy hats. "The place is like a hive of activity when all our guests are here."

"Hives is one good word to describe the place," Darren muttered and felt a foot kick him in the leg.

"I hear that there's another country legend staying here at the moment," Nesta said, sipping on her stewed tea.

Anwen rolled her eyes. "Who, Nick Franklin?" She scoffed. "I would hardly call *that* man a legend. He's got some talent, certainly. But he's no Dale Benham."

They all turned to see that the musician was standing in the doorway. He lowered his hat and offered them all a sheepish wave. "Morning, all! Don't mind me." Nick made his way to one of the empty tables and plonked himself down. Nesta hoped that he hadn't heard what Anwen had said, but, judging by the man's deflated posture, she was quite certain that he had.

"Do you remember much about Dale's last day?" Nesta asked, turning back to Anwen. "I mean, the last day you saw him?"

Anwen lowered her teapot and gave a solemn nod. "He'd been out all day and came back in around tea time. My son, Kris, was in the living room fixing one of the light switches. Dale asked if he could borrow a length of wire."

"Wire?" asked Nesta.

"Don't ask me," said Anwen with a shrug. "He said something about fixing one of his amplifiers. Anyway, my son was happy to oblige and managed to find some next door. The two got on quite well, you see. They even had a couple of drinks together in this very room once Kris had finished his jobs." She thought about her son and grinned. "He's very handy like that, my Kris. He's a good lad."

She would let herself be the judge of that, Nesta thought. "So was Kris the last person to see him that evening?"

"Oh, no. It was me." Anwen uttered her words as though she was proud of it.

Darren raised his eyebrow and made sure Nesta saw it.

"Dale would often text me if he needed anything," Anwen continued. "I'm not on call for all my guests like that, but Dale was different. He asked me for a nice cup of coffee."

"What time was this?" asked Nesta.

"About ten o'clock."

"*Ten*?!" Nesta shook her head in disgust. How anyone could imagine drinking coffee at that time of night was beyond her. Even a tea after four in the afternoon was enough to disrupt *her* sleep. "That seems quite late."

Anwen shrugged. "He was a big coffee drinker, you see. So I wasn't surprised. He was literally climbing into bed in his pyjamas when I arrived."

Nesta and Darren both looked at each other.

"He was going to bed?" asked Darren.

Anwen gave him a scowl. "A very sensible time, too, I might add. I hope your bedtime is the same."

"But he was found lying in the middle of Barmouth Bridge the next morning," Darren snapped. "I didn't read anything about him wearing pyjamas."

His host had an urge to pour the contents of her hot teapot right over his head. "Yes, well. I saw what I saw. And I can tell the time perfectly well."

"Darren has a point," said Nesta. "It's a little strange, don't you think? You must have been as surprised as we are when you heard that he was found dead — almost a mile away from where you last saw him."

"Of course I was," Anwen snapped. She suddenly realised the harsh tone of her own voice and tried to cover up the outburst with a polite smile. "I'm sorry, but Dale's death has hit me very hard, as you can imagine. It's nice that my last vision of Dale is him tucked up in bed with a hot drink. I'm sure there are many people out there who would give anything to have such a memory before losing a loved one. Sadly, life doesn't always play out that way. And the last moments of a person's life can be quite tragic."

"Did you say *loved* one?" asked Nesta. "I don't mean to pry, but are you saying that you were in love with Dale Benham?"

Anwen sighed. "Yes, as a matter of fact, I was. As was any other true fan of his music. We all loved Dale."

Nesta nodded and tried to hide her disappointment. She watched her host head off into the next room, humming a song that she recognised from Dale's *Greatest Hits* album.

"Just when you think that woman can't get any stranger," said Darren, chewing on his bacon. "It's hard enough when she *doesn't* like you. I can't imagine what it was like for that Dale Benham. I should count myself lucky."

The two guests continued the rest of their breakfast in silence (not that it took long before they gave up on their re-heated fry-up).

"Don't take it personally," Nick Franklin called out from the table nearby. "This place isn't exactly famous for its customer service."

"What exactly *is* it famous for?" asked Darren.

The musician stopped to think about it. "Deceased country singers?" Nick shook his head and took another mouthful of scrambled egg. "Doesn't bode well for me, I guess."

"My friend was telling me all about you," Nesta called back. "Country prince of the North West?"

Nick smiled and pointed his fork towards Darren. "He's a smart lad, that one. Surely you didn't need *him* to tell you that?"

Nesta smiled and headed over to join the man. "Sounds like you learnt from the best."

The singer nodded and almost caused his cowboy hat to fall straight into his plate of food. "Good old Dale. May he rest in peace."

"You and Dale must have been quite close," said Nesta. "Did you notice he was off, at all? You know, in the days leading up to his death?"

Nick chuckled. "Who, Dale? That man never gave anything away. He was a fine poker player. Dale lived life on the edge. He seemed to laugh in the face of death almost on a daily basis."

"What do you mean by that?" Nesta watched the man's smile disappear, and he looked up at her for the first time.

"You know how it is," said Nick. "Country singers are known for their wild lifestyles. People don't change all that much."

"Are you talking about alcohol?"

"Amongst other things, sure. Alcohol was a big one. But music wasn't the only thing he taught me back in the day."

"So drugs?"

Nick held up his hands. "Hey, I'm not the guy's mother. All I know is that he was a big party animal in his youth. I can't say that I've actually seen him take anything in recent years, but you can always tell."

"How was his state of mind the day before he died?" Nesta asked. "Did he seem intoxicated?"

The man stared at her, suspiciously, before laughing and turning to Darren. "Is she being serious? You never told me that your friend's a police detective." He turned back to face Nesta, who was still studying his expression.

"I'm just a fan," she said. "A fan who wants to find out the truth."

Nick began chopping up his breakfast. "Good luck to you. There's only one person who knows the truth."

Nesta tilted her head and gave him an intrigued stare. "Oh? And who's that?"

"The man they found lying on that bridge. Dale Benham was a complicated person. I don't think he ever fully understood himself." Nick munched on a mouthful of beans. "Hey! If you're a fan of country music, you should come down to the show tonight." He reached for the guitar case underneath his table and pulled out a pile of posters. Nick was preparing for another day of fierce marketing, which involved getting his flyers in as many windows as he could possibly find (often without permission).

"The Craig Tavern," Nesta muttered. She remembered that name. "Is this where the festival is being held?"

"The festival takes place all over town," said Nick. "We've got every type of venue you can imagine. But this is one of our more popular ones."

Nesta read through the line-up of musicians she had never heard of. "You seem to be the headline act."

Nick was like a Cheshire Cat with a bowl of cream. "Some might say that's where I belong. I'm not going to lie — I'm a little nervous. It's been a while. It's one of the last gigs before the festival's main event — *The Barmouth Bash* — at *The Mountain Theatre* on Saturday."

Darren leant over to look at the flyer in Nesta's hand. "What makes that night so special? Isn't it all the same acts?"

The musician laughed. "Are you kidding? *The Barmouth Bash* is the festival's main showcase. Only the best acts are selected, and everyone in town will be there. Not just country music fans. It's when our little festival goes mainstream, you could say." He looked around the room (not that there was anyone else there) and gave them a cheeky smirk. "I also happen to know that a certain record label owner will be in attendance. Cliff Booth of

Rooftop Records has produced some of the hottest albums in the last decade."

"Why would they be interested in country western singers?" asked Darren.

Nick clapped his hands and turned to Nesta. "This kid is a right card. I can never tell if he's being serious." He slapped Darren on the back. "Country music is huge again, baby! It's no surprise. The genre's been around forever, and, every decade or so, someone comes along and smashes it back into the spotlight. It never goes away."

"Like Dolly Parton?" asked Nesta.

"Uh, sure." Nick tried not to look too surprised at her first choice of artist.

"I do love a bit of Dolly." Nesta tapped her feet. "Everyone loves her." She pointed at Darren and whispered. "Don't worry, he won't know who Dolly is."

Darren frowned as the other two giggled. "Sounds like a sheep to me."

Nesta took another look at the poster. "So this *Barmouth Bash* could be your big break, then?"

Nick coughed. "Second break, to be precise. I'm hoping for something of a Nick Franklin renaissance. Something to reach a whole new generation."

"Good luck with that," said Darren.

"Don't you worry," said Nesta, giving him a nudge. "Darren and I will be at both events."

The teenager glared at her. "We *will*?"

The excited musician shook their hands. "I appreciate your support. Hey!" He pulled out some more flyers. "Any chance you guys could spread some of these around for me? Will be good to get some more tourists in."

"Absolutely." Nesta smiled. "We'll be more than happy to help."

Darren folded up his arms in a sulk. His little holiday had not got off to the best start so far, and, judging by the flyer in his hand, it wasn't about to get much better.

CHAPTER 7

Darren removed his trainer and shook out a pile of sand. He stood back up in his jeans and hoodie and looked around at all the happy holidaymakers. The sheer brightness of the large beach in the midday sun caused him to squint like a lost mole, and he was desperate to make a return to solid pavement.

"Come on!" Nesta called out. She was following an excited Hari towards the water's edge and had practically been dragging the teenager towards the sea. She wasn't a beach person herself, but this stubborn young man was something else. "You might need to roll up your trouser legs once we get there."

"There's no way I'm stepping foot in there," said Darren, as he approached, pointing towards the crashing waves. "I don't see why we can't just walk along the promenade."

Nesta breathed in a lungful of salty air. "Because we're in Barmouth! How often do you find yourself by the seaside?"

Darren didn't even need to think about it. "Never. And I can see everything just fine from over there." He turned her attention to the enormous car park. "What difference does walking through the sand make? Apart from making me more uncomfortable..."

"You couldn't look more uncomfortable if you tried," said Nesta, glancing down at his clothes. "Did you not think to pack some shorts? Maybe a pair of sandals?"

The teenager scoffed. "There's no way I'm wearing sandals. And nobody looks good in shorts."

"What about Roger Federer?" Nesta saw the same blank expression that she always received when referencing someone famous. But, unless the person was a third of her age or an internet influencer, the young man didn't have the foggiest. "It'll do you good to get some sun on you. Once you feel that sea water between your toes, you'll soon see the advantages of being in the moment."

Darren shook his head. "Sorry — not happening. No chance."

Moments later, and the teenager was crying out at the top of his lungs.

"It's bloody freezing!" he cried, jumping around in the water. "What part of this is supposed to be fun?"

An amused Nesta was finding the whole experience very pleasurable indeed, especially whilst watching him squirm around as another wave came in. She pointed towards Hari, who was in his element, splashing around in the shallow water. "You see him? That dog doesn't have another care in the world right now. He's having the time of his life. You don't see him complaining about the cold."

"That doesn't make him right," Darren snapped. "This is a person who likes a bowl of tinned meat for breakfast."

"You'll thank me later." Nesta was determined not to have her moment of zen ruined by her complaining companion and turned around to admire the scenery.

The town of Barmouth was being blessed by a period of

sunshine, and she took in the panoramic view. To the right were the steep rock faces of the Cadair Idris mountain, and below those, she could make out the timber bridge that stretched out across the estuary. Next, she turned her attention to the surrounding hills of "Old Barmouth" and struggled to make out the exterior of her accommodation. She knew it was there, watching her every move, but her eyesight was not what it used to be.

After Darren had expressed his concerns over catching hypothermia, they made their way back towards the promenade and headed past a row of food establishments and amusement arcades.

"Do you reckon that's safe?" Darren asked.

Nesta turned to see a small rollercoaster. "Probably safer than most of those fairground rides."

"What makes you say that?"

They heard a series of screams, as the runaway train made its descent.

"Nobody's taking it apart and reassembling it every few days — like the ones you see at Bala Fair. All it takes is someone forgetting a few screws or a bolt. Some of those fairground workers that I see passing through don't seem all that thorough to me."

Darren snorted out a laugh. "Fancy a ride on this one, then?"

"No chance!"

The disappointed teenager took a deep sigh and bid farewell to the most interesting part of town he had seen so far. He had hoped to spend the next couple of hours trying out the arcade games or making some money on the penny-pushers. But it seemed Nesta had other plans.

"I know a ride we can go on," said Nesta, as they turned right towards the main high street. "There's a lovely little steam train that goes from Fairbourne. I used to take the children on it when they were young. They also had a miniature railway. Maybe we should see if it's still there?"

Darren chuckled before he realised that she was being quite serious. "Why would we want to go on a steam train when we can go on one of those?"

They walked across a busy level crossing and saw a diesel train approaching. Its glowing lights were almost haunting, as it waited for the pedestrians to cross this Cambrian Coast line. Nesta and Darren made it to the other side and watched the barriers drop to the sound of a loud bell.

"You think *that* monstrosity has the charm of a little steam train?" asked Nesta. "Not all modern technology is better, you know."

"It's more practical," Darren muttered, his eyes following the train before it pulled into the station. "Is this the same line that crosses the bridge?"

Nesta nodded. In that moment, she couldn't help but imagine Dale witnessing that same locomotive heading past on the night he died. Those two headlights would surely have been blinding in the darkness and the sound of a train horn gave her a chill.

Once they had reached the high street, the mood was lifted by the sight of pubs, cafés and a wide range of independent shops, selling everything from beach equipment to crafts and homeware. It was even prettier than Nesta had remembered and had a unique sense of colour and atmosphere amongst these historic buildings.

Darren was surprised by the amount of galleries in town and grew tempted by a series of bakeries and sweet shops.

"Nick said the place was down this road," said Nesta, leading the way. She was referring to the local café that their fellow lodger had recommended back at the guesthouse, an establishment that apparently offered a generous discount to festival attendees (as well as the best cooked breakfast in town).

It may have been a little late for breakfast by the time Nesta and Darren had arrived, but they needed *something* to make up for the abysmal offerings at *Bryn Lodge*.

Unlike some of the more modern eating establishments in town, *The Cornel Café* had all the makings of a traditional greasy spoon and made little effort to stand out. In many ways, it didn't need to. The food spoke for itself, and the café already had a good reputation for serving a solid hearty breakfast that filled the stomach of every customer.

Nesta took in the comforting smells of sizzling bacon and frying bread, as she entered through the front door with a smile on her face. Finally, the chance for a proper cooked breakfast, she thought, glancing up at the small clock on the wall — *eleven o'clock* (not time for lunch, yet).

"Bore da!" cried Sandy, the café's proud hostess. "Come in, come in! Table for two?"

The woman already had the menus in her hands, and her enormous smile pushed up a pair of rosy cheeks.

"We won't be needing those," said Nesta with a chuckle. "I'll be having the Full Welsh Breakfast with a cup of tea, please."

"I'll definitely be needing one," said Darren, gladly taking his menu.

Nesta turned to their host and whispered. "He'll probably be a while deciding. Quite fussy, you see. Best tell the kitchen to start on mine."

Sandy chuckled and escorted her customers to their table. It was hard not to notice the handful of cowboy hats dotted around, as both country singers and fans alike dined on their meals to the sound of Willie Nelson playing on the radio.

"I see you've fully embraced the festival," said Nesta, as she sat down.

"'Tis the season," said Sandy with a giggle and pointed up at her own cowboy hat. "The café's a proud sponsor, you see. Hence all the flyers everywhere — and the discount."

"Is this *your* café?" Nesta asked. She was quite impressed with the customer service so far, something which didn't always accompany a greasy spoon.

Sandy clutched her chest. "Alas, I'm afraid not. That would be our lord and master over at the stove. Isn't that right, Hywel?!"

"Hey?!" a scruffy man in a stained apron called back from behind the stove.

"Just saying how friendly and cheerful you are!" Sandy called out again before turning back to her customers. "He can't hear a thing back there. Just as well, probably." She lifted up her notepad and pen. "I'm Sandy, by the way. I'll be your waitress today." The woman giggled. "All this country music makes me feel like I'm working in one of those American diners. I should get one of those coffee pots and walk around topping people up."

Nesta smiled. "Sandy... that's an unusual name."

The café worker rolled her eyes. "That's my mother for you. Big *Grease* fan. Still, could have been worse. She also liked *Dirty Dancing!*"

"Oh, heavens!" Nesta couldn't help but giggle. "Good job you didn't put us in the corner, baby!"

The two women smirked at each other, as an utterly confused Darren looked on. "Uh, can I order now?"

"Of course you can, young man!" Sandy lifted up her pad. "Fire away!"

"I'll have just the sausages. With the toast on the side. Not a sandwich, like."

Nesta coughed. "Like I said — very fussy."

"Splendid choice," said Sandy. The hostess was about to head off, when Nesta couldn't help but ask her about the man behind the stove. He had enormous side burns and appeared to be singing away to the song on the radio.

"Tell me," she said. "Is your boss something of a performer?"

Sandy was slightly taken aback. "Why, yes. How did you know that?"

"I can tell these things." Nesta rested her elbows against the table and smiled. "I can also spot a budding entertainer from a mile away. I've met more than my fair share."

"Oh, he's more than just a *budding* singer," said Sandy. She leant forward and lowered her voice. "He does gigs and everything. Thinks he's a proper Keith Urban. Only without the stunning good looks and Australian accent. Which is a shame if you ask me."

"Why such a shame?" asked Nesta. "That he *performs*?"

Sandy gave her a playful wink. "I was talking about the stunning good looks." She let out a mischievous grin and headed off to another table.

Darren sighed. "She was a bit much," he said. "All I wanted was some toast and a couple of sausages. Why is everyone in this town such hard work?"

"I rather like her," said Nesta. "You just need to cheer up, you miserable sod. You're worse than my late husband sometimes." She took another look at Hywel, the owner. He was still swanning around in front of his stove as if it were an audience. Nesta hoped that the man could cook a lot better than he could sing, or they were in a lot of trouble.

CHAPTER 8

Nesta and Darren followed the narrow, curved path leading to the swing bridge looming in the distance. This steel structure hovered over the Mawddach waters and was the first section before the half-mile timber crossing that carried thousands of pedestrians a year. To their right was the empty railway line which reminded Nesta of her many walks along the tracks of the *Bala Lake Railway*. Her local steam train felt like a miniature model compared to this impressive piece of engineering.

"It clearly wasn't suicide," Darren muttered.

Nesta turned to her walking companion with a confused frown. "What do you mean?"

"Dale's death. We can rule out the fact that he might have killed himself."

"How can you be so sure?"

Darren turned her attention to their surroundings. "Look at this place. If you didn't fancy jumping into the estuary, you could just throw yourself in front of a passing train. But he didn't do any of those."

Nesta sighed, even though she knew he had a point. "It's frightening how your mind works, sometimes."

They crossed over onto the timber walkway, and the teenager began trying to hide his nerves. "I hope this thing is safe."

"This bridge has been around long before you were born," said Nesta.

"That's exactly what I'm afraid of," said Darren, keeping himself away from the edge. "It's probably rotting away as we speak. This thing could go at any minute."

"Well, we better get a move on, then." Nesta lifted up her binoculars and pointed them towards the west side of the bridge. She spotted a small ferry chugging its way towards the harbour. If she remembered rightly, that was the crossing a person could take after a trip on the *Fairbourne Railway*.

"We can't be far from the halfway mark now," she said after a good ten minutes of walking.

"It's about another minute," said Darren.

Nesta turned to see that he was staring down at his mobile phone to track their progress. "If you don't watch where you're going, then you'll end up in the water," she snapped. "Or maybe I'll throw that thing in first."

Her threat caused the teenager to look up in horror, and he reluctantly put the phone away. "I thought you wanted to work out how long it would have taken Dale to walk to the middle?"

"I don't need a satellite navigation device to tell me that. We're walking it now, aren't we?"

Darren wanted to ridicule her for the use of the words " satellite navigation", but he preferred to stay dry. "Maybe he was robbed," he said.

"It's a strange place to rob someone," said Nesta, gazing around at the vast open space. "A meeting point would be more likely."

"You think he was meeting the person who ended up killing him?"

Nesta shrugged. "Depends on who he was meeting."

They reached (what Darren had determined to be) the halfway point and spotted a figure up in the distance. Hari began barking at the sight of a German Shepherd, who looked like he could have eaten the little Jack Russell for breakfast.

"Hari!" Nesta shouted. "Stop it!"

"He's braver than me," said Darren, slowing his pace at the sight of the large dog. "I wouldn't want a fight with that thing."

The German Shepherd's owner was leaning against the handrail with a fishing rod in his hand. The man had a hard face with stubble as rough as sand paper. He was no stranger to the outdoors and looked like he would be quite comfortable doing the same thing in the harshest of weather conditions.

Hari continued his barking frenzy, until the German Shepherd silenced him with a single bark of his own.

"That'll teach you," Nesta told her Jack Russell, as they approached the fisherman. "You need to know your place."

"Quiet, Shelley!" The man called Rhys shook his head. "You'll scare the fish."

Nesta stopped walking. "I'm sorry, that's Hari's fault. Your dog has a lot of patience."

"Don't worry about it," said Rhys. The man had a rolled-up cigarette drooping out of the side of his lips.

"Shelley's a nice name." Nesta gave the German Shepherd a stroke (much to the disapproval of Hari).

"She used to love chewing on shells when she was a puppy. So Shelley seemed appropriate enough." Rhys spoke with a husky voice that reminded Darren of his uncle. He was a man who enjoyed his own company but at that moment wasn't given much choice.

"Have you caught anything yet?" Nesta asked, peering over

the side. Her question naturally aggravated the unlucky fisherman.

"Not yet," Rhys muttered. "But I'm in no rush."

Nesta glanced down at the bait in his bucket. "You seem like you're after more than crabs." She had already walked past several people at the harbour dropping their buckets into the water. Crab fishing had been high on the list when she was visiting as a little girl, and her father sometimes used to bring fresh crabs home to Bala if he had been travelling anywhere near the area. She could still taste them now.

"I'd like to get me a nice salmon," said Rhys. "But I'll more likely get a Sea Trout if I'm lucky."

"What if you catch nothing?" asked Darren.

The man slowly turned his head and let out a smile. "Then it would have still been a good day."

Darren was not as optimistic. He hated the thought of fishing and could never imagine lasting ten minutes staring into space. At the very least, he would need a podcast. "I don't know how you do it."

Nesta was about to snap at the young man, when Rhys turned back to look at him. "It takes practise, lad, like anything else."

"*Practise*? For doing nothing?"

"*Especially* for doing nothing." Rhys stared at him and pointed at his own head. "The mind needs to be tamed. It can be wild like the sea. When you calm it down, everything becomes clear."

Darren was slightly disturbed by the stranger's cryptic words and wished he had never asked the question. "Yeah, I suppose I know what you mean. I get the same thing when I'm watching telly."

Rhys let out a croaky laugh. "You should try it some day." He looked back out at the estuary. "Just take a moment to sit with

your own thoughts for half an hour and take in your surroundings. I do it every single day."

"Do you come *here* every day?" asked Nesta.

The man gave his German Shepherd a stroke. "Me and
Shelley walk this bridge twice a day. Rain or shine. She needs a
decent walk, and it keeps me healthy."

Nesta nodded. "Dogs are good for that. I take my Hari to the
edge of Llyn Tegid every day."

"Bala, eh?" Rhys seemed to approve and pointed in the direction of Fairbourne. "I have a house about twenty minutes from
here. Nice and quiet. Just how I like it."

"You must have heard about what happened to the country
singer here recently," said Nesta.

"Oh, aye." Rhys pointed further down the bridge. "They
found his body right up there. This whole area was blocked off
not that long ago. There was no walk for me and Shelley on *those*
days."

"Did you get to see anything?" asked Darren.

Rhys saw the teenager's curiosity and smiled. "Did I see the
body, you mean? I bet you'd like to hear all the gory details,
wouldn't you?"

Darren shrugged. "Sure, why not?"

Nesta decided to interject. "Did anything else look out of the
ordinary?"

"What, apart from a dead person in the middle of the bridge,
you mean?" He chuckled. "Don't see that every morning, that's
for sure."

His evasiveness was already starting to get on Nesta's nerves.
"What I mean is — were the police looking like they found
anything else? Like a piece of evidence?"

Rhys chuckled again. "You're asking like it was a game of
Cluedo. Like a police officer was holding up an evidence bag
with a revolver inside."

A murder weapon would have been quite handy, Nesta thought. "Sounds like you didn't see all that much." She was about to bid him farewell, when he spoke again.

"It's pretty hard to have a good nosey when the police are trying to question you."

Nesta's disappointment vanished. "They questioned you?"

"Course," said Rhys, as though it were perfectly normal. "I was probably the last person to see the guy alive."

Nesta and Darren both looked at each other and waited for him to elaborate.

"I was getting a walk in that night," Rhys continued. "Me and Shelley often do a late one these days. It's quite peaceful after the sun goes down, and all you can hear out here is the water splashing." He pointed in the direction of the Barmouth side of the bridge. "We'd made it right to the end when I saw him."

"Dale Benham?" asked Darren.

Rhys stared at him. "How does a guy your age know who Dale Benham is?"

"He's got exquisite taste," said Nesta with a smile."

"Anyway," said Rhys. "There he was, coming towards us. I'd met him a couple of times, actually. He used to like crossing this bridge. I first saw him at a gig in town years ago. It was a good night, and I went to shake his hand after the show. Good bloke."

"Did he say anything when you passed him?" asked Nesta.

Rhys shook his head. "Didn't have time."

"He was in a hurry? Did he walk straight past you?"

The man gave her a confused frown. "*Walked*?" He looked at her as though she was losing her mind. "He wasn't walking." He paused, whilst the other two were completely flummoxed. "He was riding a bike."

CHAPTER 9

The walk to the other end of Barmouth Bridge had been a silent one. After the conversation with the man who had claimed to be the last person to see Dale Benham alive, Nesta and Darren were lost in their own thoughts. Neither of them had pictured the singer cycling across the bridge in the dead of night, and his mode of transport added a whole new layer to this peculiar mystery.

They both stared down at the wooden boards passing beneath their feet, almost hypnotising them into a dreamy trance. The rest of the bridge had looked exactly the same with its repetitive fencing and endless railway track, which continued on into the distance as though it would never end. Reaching the other side, they found a narrow footpath surrounded by grass. The railway line was still present only a few feet away, but they were now very much walking on solid ground.

"How long does this path go for?" asked Darren.

Nesta shrugged. "There's only one way to find out."

Darren looked at her with sheer reluctance. "Haven't we walked enough?"

"You heard what the man said," said Nesta. "It sounds like Dale covered a lot of ground on that bicycle of his."

According to Rhys, Dale's bicycle had been found in a ditch further along the very same path they were now treading.

"That doesn't mean that Dale went this far," said Darren.

"No, but the killer did." Nesta looked over at the upcoming fields and trees in the distance. "Whover killed Dale decided that he needed to dispose of the bike. Why? And why head all the way back this way to get rid of it when they were quite happy to leave his body on the bridge?"

Darren shook his head. "Because they were a crazy killer. And crazy killers do crazy things."

Nesta shook her head. "It sounds like the killer was heading back in this direction."

"You reckon?"

"Why not dispose of the bike on the Barmouth side? That man on the bridge didn't say exactly where the bike was ditched."

"Maybe the killer was using the bike to escape."

"Exactly," said Nesta. "He or she was likely using it to get home. Otherwise they would have to go back and cross the bridge again. Too risky."

Darren took another look around at their surroundings. There wasn't an awful lot to see, apart from fields of sheep and the estuary behind them. "You think the killer lived out here?"

"Let's keep going," said Nesta.

They kept walking in the direction of the distant hills. These great mounds were miles away with their layers of trees.

Nesta pointed towards the wide open space over to the right. "There's a golf course up that way. Morgan once dragged me across nine holes. I was absolutely done for, but the view was stunning."

The teenager had no interest in golf and couldn't think of

anything worse than walking around a course for hours on end, trying to pot a ball. He had played a video game version once and that had been painful enough)but at least it hadn't required walking great distances like they were now).

"How much further?" he asked after another twenty minutes. "My feet are killing me."

Nesta continued her determined strides. Rhys, the fisherman on the bridge, had said that Dale Benham's bicycle had been found in a ditch near a sign for *Morwyn Farm*, and she was keen on finding out how far his mode of transport had travelled that night.

"Here it is," said Nesta after another ten minutes of complaining from her companion.

They approached a wooden sign that was barely hanging from its posts. The name *Morwyn Farm* had been carved into the surface and was fading after decades of abuse from heavy rain. "This is where someone must have dumped the bike."

Darren stared down at the muddy ditch in front of a crumbling drystone wall. "What if it was the other way around?" He turned to a confused Nesta.

"How do you mean?"

"Well," said Darren, who was rather proud of his new theory, "maybe they didn't kill Dale on the bridge then dump the bike here. Maybe they killed Dale on his bike, right here, and then dragged his body to the bridge."

Nesta stared at him in disbelief. "Why on earth would they do it *that* way around?"

Darren smiled. "Exactly! To put us all off the scent."

"I think you've had too much salty air," said Nesta. "That's the most ridiculous thing I've ever heard."

Darren frowned. "Alright — fine. I'll let you tell me a better idea."

Nesta watched her Jack Russell, sniffing away in the ditch.

"I'd say our killer is a lot more lazy than that." She pointed to the sign. "They more likely used his bike to get home and dumped it before they got there."

"No way. Nobody's *that* stupid." He saw the way she was looking at him and could see where her mind was going. "Don't even say it."

Nesta restrained herself from giving him a good example and headed through the opening of a dirt track beside the sign.

"Where are you going now?" Darren asked.

"Where do you think?" she asked, summoning her dog. "To see if anyone's home!"

The teenager took another look around at the rural surroundings and wanted to remind her that they were in the middle of nowhere. The last thing he wanted to do was visit the house of a potential killer, where the nearest signs of intelligent life had four legs and a woolly coat.

Morwyn Farm was a modest holding, consisting of an old barn, a handful of outbuildings and a cottage made of local stone. The main yard was empty when Nesta and her reluctant follower entered its small space. They could still see the same foothills of the Cadair Idris mountains as they could from Barmouth Beach, as well as the Mawddach Estuary they had headed away from, which seemed smaller now from this lonely property.

"Can I help you?" asked a man in Wellington boots. Gethin Moore was a young farmer, and he rarely saw people passing through his farmyard. "You look a bit lost."

Nesta turned around, trying not to appear startled. Darren also turned around, making no effort to hide his surprise, whatsoever. "No, we're definitely not lost." He had seen enough horror films to make the mistake of using *that* word.

"Ah," said Nesta, marching over to shake the man's hand. "So, you're the farmer."

Gethin accepted the woman's gesture with great suspicion. "Sure. I'm the farmer. How ever did you guess?"

"It's a lovely farm you've got here." Nesta took another look around his yard. "I grew up on a farm, you see. But we certainly didn't have a sea view."

"I'm sorry," said Gethin. "And who are you, exactly? Because if you're another one of those journalists, you can sod off. I don't know nothing about that country western guy."

"Oh, I'm sorry." She marched over to shake his hand again. "I'm Nesta from Bala."

The man waited for her to elaborate, but he got nothing. "So what are you trying to sell me?"

"Sell?" Nesta chuckled. "I'm no good at selling. I tried opening a market stall once and that didn't go too well."

The farmer turned to Darren. "Is your granny alright?"

The teenager sighed. "She's not my —"

"Granny?!" Nesta entered the man's space and caused him to take a step back. "Now see here, young man. I didn't come here criticising *your* age."

"What do mean — my age?"

Nesta stepped back and gave his appearance another inspection. "Well, look at you. You're far too young to be a farmer. You seem better suited to a catwalk than shearing sheep. Let me guess — are the wellies just for show? Or is it your father actually running this place?"

"My father's dead," said Gethin.

There was a long silence in the yard.

"Oh," said Nesta. She was now regretting her sudden outburst. "I'm sorry to hear that."

Gethin was almost amused by her change in tone. "Yep, it's just me, myself and I down here. Mam upped and left one Christmas when I was a kid. I chose to stay and have barely seen her since."

Nesta found his casual demeanour uncomfortable, and she could tell that he was enjoying it. "So you have to run this whole farm yourself?"

The young man pulled out a pack of cigarettes and shrugged. "Doesn't bother me. I was doing it long before dad died. He lost the use of his legs, see. Couldn't even stand up by the end, the poor sod. Horrible disease he had."

"How long ago was this?" Nesta asked.

"A few years ago," said Gethin. "I'd say my life is easier now that I don't need to take care of him."

Nesta turned to look at Darren, who still looked uneasy.

"I think it's time we headed back," said the teenager. He gave Nesta an assertive stare and turned to walk away. "Uh, yes. I suppose we better had. Sorry to have disturbed you." She searched for Hari and saw him sniffing against a shed door. "Come on, Hari!" As Nesta crossed the yard, her instincts caused her to pause. "Can I just ask you something?"

Gethin blew out a lungful of smoke. "Here we go. Is it about my double glazing?"

"You mentioned the country singer," said Nesta. "They found his bicycle near your farm."

The farmer smiled. "So I heard. What's that got to do with you?"

"I could ask you the same thing."

Gethin laughed. "You're something else, aren't you? You think that has something to do with me? I wasn't even home that night. I was at a poker tournament in Blackpool. A solid alibi."

Darren had stopped walking and was losing his patience. "Are we going now or what?"

The farmer blew out another puff of smoke. "Have you really come to my property so you can accuse me of being linked with that cowboy singer? I don't know how they do things in Bala, but, over here, we mind our own business."

"I'm not accusing you of anything," said Nesta. "I'm just trying to get to the bottom of what happened."

"Who are you? His mother?"

"Just a fan. Or at least... my husband was, anyway."

"A fan?" Gethin scoffed. "People actually *like* that honky tonk stuff?" He shook his head and finished the rest of his cigarette. "I've not got a clue about the bike. Someone was probably trying to frame me, knowing the locals. I'm hardly that popular. I knew who the Dale bloke was, like. Used to see him down the golf club when he was in town."

"He used to play golf?" Nesta thought about the unique course only a couple of miles from where they were standing.

"Not very well," said Gethin. "We don't get many yanks round here, and he stood out like a sore thumb. Could spot him a mile off with his cowboy hat."

"How would you rate your own golfing skills?"

Gethin shrugged. "I'm alright. I got a twelve handicap. So probably about average."

"Not bad," said Nesta. She bid the man a farewell and joined Darren on the other side of the yard.

"He's definitely a psychopath," said the teenager once they were heading back towards the bridge. "That's the second one I've seen today, counting our host. Dale didn't stand a chance in this town."

Nesta was still deep in thought and barely acknowledged his remark. Gethin had certainly given off a suspicious energy, but, in her eyes, that didn't make him a killer. Living in isolation did strange things to a person. Her main takeaway from their brief conversation was Gethin's assumption that he had been framed. The farmer clearly thought that someone was out to get him. If there was one thing she could be certain of in a small community like this one, it was that she would have no trouble finding out the reason.

CHAPTER 10

The *Craig Tavern* was a little harder to find than some of Barmouth's more popular local pubs. But the fact that it hadn't even featured on Darren's online map did not discourage these two visitors from Bala. They had already returned to their accommodation to freshen up and were now making their way through the creaky front doors with an open mind.

Nesta had not attended a country and western music festival before, and she was curious to find out what this one had to offer.

The music had been loud enough for them to hear it from outside the pub, and they were both expecting a room full of people engaging in a traditional barn dance. What they found instead was an almost empty bar room with only a handful of die-hard enthusiasts dotted around the room. The couple on the small stage were singing their own rendition of a Johnny and June Carter Cash song, only they shared a closer resemblance to Paul Daniels and Debbie McGee.

"It's not too late to go somewhere else," Darren muttered, as they entered.

"You made it!" cried an excited voice.

Nick Franklin had his guitar in one hand and a pint of beer in the other. "You're just in time — Simon and Julie have a couple of songs left. They're my warm-up act tonight. It's getting busier now."

Nesta and Darren looked around at the small turn out and wondered whether they were looking at the same room.

"Is this a good example of a usual evening at the festival?" Nesta asked. She couldn't help but notice the elderly man in the corner who was fast asleep.

Nick nodded. "I'd say this is a pretty good crowd tonight. Sometimes it's a bit quieter for the matinees." The two people opposite him looked very concerned.

"I think we should probably get ourselves a drink," said Nesta. "You probably need to get ready."

The singer laughed and raised up his pint of ale. "I'm always ready! Performing comes natural. I guess it's in the blood." He pointed to the bar. "Tell them you're with me, and they'll do you some freebies."

"Oh," said Nesta (who always enjoyed a good freebie). "That's very kind." She walked Darren to the bar and found a grumpy-looking bartender. "I'll have a glass of red and a *Coke* for my young friend here."

The bartender took his time providing the drinks and punched a few numbers into his till. "That'll be eight-fifty."

Nesta leant forward with an excited grin. "Actually, we're with Mr Franklin."

"Who?"

She pointed to the singer, who was busy dancing in front of his warm-up act in a gesture of support.

"You mean — Nick?" The bartender frowned. "It's about time someone paid off his tab. He owes me a fortune."

Nesta was now struck by a rush of panic. "Oh, no! I didn't

mean I was clearing his tab. He said there might be some complimentary drinks?"

"Complimentary?" The bartender laughed. "He's a right joker. Now that's ten-fifty, please."

"I thought you said eight-fifty?" Darren asked.

The man turned to the teenager. "Oh, you're paying, are you, lad?"

Darren kept his mouth shut and waited for Nesta to hand over her money.

They both headed to the other side of the bar and grabbed some stools.

A man in a cheap suit was perched nearby with his arms folded. Robin Lock had a bald head that was wrinkled by his harsh frown. "I'd go somewhere else if I were you," he muttered.

A curious Nesta turned to the man. "You're not enjoying yourself?"

Robin swallowed the rest of his whiskey and scoffed. "Believe me," he said, "I'm not here for pleasure."

"I don't mean to be nosey," said Nesta. "But why exactly *are* you here?"

The talent agent pointed to the couple on the stage. "They're my act."

"*Your* act?"

Robin nodded. "I'm their manager. In fact, I manage most of the performers in this festival."

Nesta took another look around the quiet pub. Judging by the poor turnout, she suspected that the man was hardly raking in the money. "Anyone I would have heard of?"

"Probably not," said Robin. "My most famous client is now dead."

The red wine trickled down Nesta's throat, and she felt a warmth in the pit of her stomach. "You represented Dale Benham?"

The manager sighed and hated being reminded. "He was the first country western singer on my books. Sadly, he wasn't the last."

"You don't like country music? And you manage people like *these* two?" Nesta watched the couple wail into their microphones. "Seems a little strange."

"Not really," Robin snapped. "People in my line of work are all about making money. It's never about the music — no matter what they tell you. Country's big again. Unfortunately for me, you wouldn't know it. Not if you saw my bank account. I should have stuck with heavy metal at this rate."

Darren's ears pricked up at the mere mention of his favourite genre. "What kind of heavy metal?"

Robin leant forward to see the curious teenager on the other side of Nesta. "I represented all sorts: Whiplash, Dragonbreath, Deathdemons..."

"You managed Deathdemons?!" Darren almost dropped his glass. "What were they like?"

"Exactly the same as any other rock group," said Robin. "Greedy, egotistical, temperamental..."

Darren smiled. "That's awesome."

"Dale Benham was different," Robin continued. "And when I saw how many records he was selling back in the day, I decided to move away from the metal and go all in on the country." He stared into his empty glass like it was a lost friend. "And look at me now."

"Dale must have made you a few Bob," said Nesta.

"Oh, yeah. Back in the day, he did. I was his only UK manager when I first signed him. He was the biggest cash cow I ever had. Never went mainstream, sadly, but he was a lot more profitable than any of those heavy metal bands. I never looked back for a long time."

"And what changed?" asked Nesta.

"The sales," Robin muttered. "In the last five years, they started dropping, rapidly. It's always my biggest fear. Sometimes you just can't control the market. And Dale Benham started to get stale. His loyal fanbase started to dwindle. The fact he stopped releasing new records didn't help."

"Why was that?"

"He stopped releasing new songs and just relied on playing the old stuff. Which was fine for the gigs, but the records were a huge stream of income for us. Then, his mother died… it was like he'd given up. His heart wasn't in the music anymore."

"Sounds like his mother meant a lot to him," said Nesta. "Grief can do a great deal of damage to a person."

Robin signalled to the barman and waved his empty glass. "Oh, he loved his mother. He used to sing to her. She was a big country fan. In many ways, I think it was his obsessive desire to impress his mother that got him into performing in the first place. I don't think he really enjoyed any of it."

Nesta listened with a heavy heart. She hated to think of a singer like Dale Benham hating his own music. He had always seemed like he enjoyed playing more than anything, and the thought of his enthusiasm being a giant act for the audience made her sick to her stomach. Morgan would have been crushed to hear that his hero was merely going through the motions. "You don't really believe that, do you?"

"Course I do," Robin said, accepting his new drink. "The minute Dale's mother died, it was like he'd lost all motivation completely." He sipped on his whiskey and smiled. "I met her once, Dale's mother. She owned a large estate in Texas. Lydia was originally from Barmouth and ended up marrying some oil tycoon out there. Sharp as they come, she was — before the dementia."

"I'm sorry to hear that," said Nesta. "It's a terrible disease."

Robin nodded. "And Lydia got it bad. It was painful to watch.

But she still liked her music. Dale never stopped playing for her."

Nesta thought about the singer, wallowing in his grief. She certainly knew how that felt. "He must have inherited a lot of money," she said, eventually. Robin gave her a cautious stare. "You said that his mother had a large estate?"

"Yes," said Robin. "I supposed he would have done." He looked up at the various audience members all dotted around the room. The manager had grown used to these numbers after the last few years, but it still troubled him. "Although, if Dale really *did* inherit all of his mother's fortune, I can't see why he bothered slumming it in venues like this for the last year of his life."

"How long ago did his mother pass away?" asked Nesta.

The man gave her question some thought. "I'd say it was just over a year ago."

Nesta saw his point. If Dale *was* a wealthy man with a large estate (and if he really *did* hate playing as much as his manager seemed to think), then it made no sense embarking on a tour that nobody seemed to be attending. Either that, or he had bigger problems. "Do you know if Dale had any large debts?"

"Debts?"

"Like you said," Nesta added, "why else would he be back on tour again?"

Robin sighed. "My clients are not my children. I'm their manager, not a carer. I couldn't care less about what they get up to in their spare time. As long as they turn up on time."

Nesta studied his mannerisms. His vague answer implied that Dale might still have been in some financial debt after all. "How much money would a festival like this bring in?"

The manager shook his head. "There's no money in this festival anymore. Not like there used to be. The whole thing's gone downhill over the years." He pointed towards a table on the other side of the pub. A large woman with an enormous amount of jewellery and make-up was howling with laughter alongside the two acquaintances on either side of her. "It doesn't help that it's being run by a festival director who treats the whole thing like her own private party."

Nia Llywelyn paid no attention to the singers on the stage, as they performed their last chorus to a room with less energy than a graveyard shift worker after a turkey dinner. Unlike her father (the founder of this annual festival), she seemed more interested in mingling with the talent over a few bottles of wine than watching them sing.

"She's running this festival into the ground," said Robin with a disgusted snarl.

"If the festival is so bad," said Nesta, "then why bother coming?"

Robin chuckled. "Good question." He swallowed another mouthful of his favourite beverage. "There's only one reason I've come back this year — and that's Cliff Booth."

Nesta recognised that name from her conversation with Nick. "The *Rooftop Records* man?"

The manager appeared to be impressed. "The one and only. Turns out he likes to take family holidays on the Welsh coast. I managed to persuade him to come down for the last night at *The Mountain Theatre*. And believe me — it took a lot of persuading!"

"I heard that he was a bit of a big cheese," said Nesta.

"Big cheese? In my world, he's a big, fat wheel of *Double Gloucester*." Robin began pondering his big opportunity. "If I can get him to sign just one of my acts, I can actually afford to retire from this blood-sucking business."

Nesta smiled. "I know all about retirement."

Robin huffed. "Unfortunalely for me, the music industry don't offer pension plans. I've got all my eggs loaded in one basket for this one."

Darren studied the couple on stage, as they bowed to a series of single claps. Surely, he thought, the man wasn't talking about *Simon and Julie*. "You mean — Nick Franklin?"

The manager almost sprayed out his mouthful of whiskey all over Nesta's face. "*Nick Franklin*?!" He let out a wicked laugh. "*That* bumbling idiot? You think I'd risk the rest of my career on *him*?"

They all turned to see that Nick was now getting ready to take over the stage. The singer seemed nervous, as he tuned his guitar with quivering hands.

"I'll give you two words," said Robin. "The Golden Wanderers."

"That's three words," Darren muttered with a cough and pointed towards Nesta. "She used to be a teacher."

Nesta appreciated the correction but couldn't help being distracted by the name. "Wait, *The Golden Wanderers*? Don't you mean — The Silver Rangers?"

Robin clapped his hands. "Aha! Not any more!" The man struggled to contain his excitement. "The Silver Rangers are dead. Long live The Gold Wanderers! Good name, eh? I came up with it myself. Talk about a new and improved version. We all know gold is better than silver."

"Wait, I don't understand..." A confused Nesta shook her head. She wanted to point out that his new and improved clients sounded more like a packet of crisps than a band, but there were more important points to discuss. "The Silver Rangers were Dale Benham's group. It's like Tom Petty and The Heartbreakers. They don't exist separately."

"They do now," said Robin. "I've re-packaged those boys as the next big thing in country music. You heard it here first. We've got a new album in the works and everything."

"How long have you been planning this for?" asked a baffled

Nesta, who didn't get the chance to have her question answered. Robin was now more preoccupied with the night's headline act.

Nick Franklin had startled the room by knocking into his microphone and almost toppling the entire stand over. He made a sheepish apology, and it soon became apparent that he was highly inebriated. "Sorry about that," he said, his voice slurring. He re-adjusted his microphone to the sound of ear-piercing feedback and prepared to start off his set with a cover of "Hey, Good Lookin'" by Hank Williams.

Robin groaned. "He never listens. I've told him a hundred times to give up this stuff."

Nesta's foot had already begun to tap. "I don't mind a bit of Hank."

"With all due respect," said the manager, "you're not really my target audience."

"How dare you!" Nesta cried.

The man held up his hands as though she were about to shoot him. "People nowadays don't want Hank. Even Shelton Williams — Hank Williams' grandson — doesn't do *Hank*! They want Luke Combs, Blake Shelton or Carrie Underwood." He glared at the man singing away on stage with sheer contempt. "I told that buffoon to evolve or die. He's obviously choosing the latter option." A pair of rowdy punters in football shirts, who clearly had not come for the country music in the first place, started wailing and heckling the singer. "But Nick wants to be like Dale. And Dale was inspired by Hank."

Nick's pre-gig beer binge was starting to take its toll, and the man was missing his notes and forgetting his lyrics. His unpolished performance was only encouraging his hecklers even more, and their chants kept causing him to lose his concentration.

"Boo!! Get off!!" The two men began throwing their beer

mats, and one of them hit Nick straight in the forehead. "You're rubbish, mate!"

The singer stopped playing and turned his attention to the two men. He grabbed hold of the microphone and pointed at them, swaying like a buoy in the wind. "Why don't you show a bit of respect?!"

"Oh, please, no..." Robin clutched his own forehead and cringed.

"You heard me!" Nick called again. "This is a Hank Williams classic!"

The two men howled with laughter, which only infuriated the singer even more.

"I'd like to see you two up here! You pair of talentless morons!"

The rowdy hecklers stopped laughing and frowned. Their tattooed forearms were beginning to flex but Nick had no intention of stopping.

"I bet you two couldn't even count to three — let alone play an instrument!" Nick took a step closer to the edge of the stage and could see the two men standing up from their chairs. "That's it! Come on then! You think I'm scared of a pair of *Chelsea* fans? I've got people in this pub who will back me up! Just you watch!" He looked over at the bar to see that his manager had already upped and left after finishing off his whiskey. The disappointment caused him to sway even more, until he lost all balance and went flying off the edge of the stage.

Nesta and Darren both winced at the man's awkward landing, and, after taking a heavy fall, Nick opened his eyes to find himself lying on the hard floor. He looked up to see a pair of bald heads with furious faces glaring down at him. The singer gave them an embarrassed smile. "You couldn't help me up, would you, lads? I think I might have twisted my ankle."

CHAPTER 11

Noel Hegarty had never had a wake-up call in his entire adult life. This was one of the many benefits of a job that required late nights and miles of travelling. So when he heard the *banging* noise against the side of his campervan that morning, he wasn't best pleased.

His fellow band member, Eric, was still snoring underneath his duvet and could sleep through a hurricane if he had to.

Noel felt the harsh sunlight against his tired face and sat up to find a woman's face in the window.

"Jesus!" he cried out, jumping out of his mattress and almost hitting his head against the ceiling. The man with wild hair and a scruffy beard leapt for the door and was ready to give this woman a piece of his mind.

Nesta was waiting for him outside his campervan, and, when he saw the tray of coffees and smelt the hot rolls, Noel hesitated.

"Good morning!" Nesta cried. "I hope you like bacon and sausages."

The man in his pyjamas stared at her, suspiciously, and saw Darren nearby with a handful of pastries. "What's all this in aid of?"

Nesta feigned an innocent response. "Oh, you know, we were just in the area and thought you might be hungry." She saw the suspicion in his face increase and smiled. "We're big fans."

Darren wanted to tell her to speak for herself but had been told to keep quiet.

Noel took another look at the free food and beverages and whistled. "Breakfast, boys!"

Eric, the largest of the group, was the first to appear. He gladly accepted his own share before retreating straight back into his bed.

"That's Eric," said Noel. "He eats, sleeps, drinks and repeats. He's bigger than his double bass these days."

The door on the second campervan flew open, and two other band members emerged in search of food.

"What we got here, then?" Drummer Stew rubbed his hands together and helped himself. He was followed by Clive, a man who seemed like he only ever came out at night and was the silent type with beady eyes.

"They're all coming out of the woodwork now," said Noel with a laugh, watching his band mates taking their food. "That's the fastest I've ever seen you two get out of bed."

Stew saluted him and returned to the confines of his van. Clive headed off across the car park and sat himself down next to a tree.

"Is that man alright?" Nesta asked. "He looks a bit unwell."

"That's just Clive," said Noel with a mouthful of bacon. "He always looks like that. The guy doesn't say much and likes to keep to himself. Sliding steel guitar players are always oddballs. You have to be, choosing an instrument like that. They're few and far between."

"Isn't that the one that makes those Hawaiian noises?" asked Nesta. She loved that sound which often reminded her of old-fashioned country music.

"Yeah, that's the one. Pretty sure it's from Hawaii, actually. Clive will tell you. You ask him about sliding steel guitars and the guy won't shut up!" Noel swallowed another mouthful and lowered his voice. "I wouldn't get too friendly, though. Legend has it Clive spent some time behind bars. Nobody seems to know why." The man shrugged. "But, hey, we needed a sliding steel guitar player, and the guy was available."

Nesta nodded and observed Clive eating his breakfast like a hunched gargoyle.

"Do all of your friends have interesting backgrounds?" she asked.

"Friends?!" Noel laughed. "I'd be a sad case to call this sorry bunch my friends. I woudn't say there's anything interesting about people who stay in a backing group all their lives. They're in the background for a reason."

"Aren't you a member of that backing group?" Darren asked.

Noel's smug demeanour vanished for a moment, and he gave the teenager a harsh stare. "Why, yes. How highly observant of you." He took a swill of coffee. "The thing is, I never intended on staying in the background. That was never part of the plan."

"Then why did you join a group called Dale Benham and The Silver Rangers?" Nesta asked. "Surely that name wasn't going to change anytime soon." She squinted at the man in his twenties. "In fact, I don't remember seeing you the last time I saw a Dale Benham gig."

The mention of his former front man caused Noel to cringe. "That's because I only joined the band a year ago. I was a replacement for Duke Phillips." He saw her thinking. "You see! I bet you didn't know that name. Fortunately, the backing members are easily replaceable. Duke was an original Silver Ranger who dropped dead one night. Dale had seen me playing at a bar in Austin. I guess you could say I was in the right place at the right time." He turned around and pointed at his campervan. "Or, depending on how you look at the last year of my life — the wrong place!" He clapped his hands and sniggered.

Nesta took a bite of one of the spare rolls and received a dirty look from Darren (he had been told that the food was strictly for the band members. "What do you mean by — your predecessor *dropped dead*?"

Noel scratched his head. "I think they said he had a heart attack or something. I forget. I guess this group has a pretty bad mortality rate if you count our former leader." He took another look back at the campervans. "Then again, I'm the only guy here who isn't pushing sixty."

"I heard that!" a voice called out from his bed.

"I thought you seemed a lot younger than the others," said Nesta, who wanted to point out that there was nothing old about "pushing sixty".

Noel nodded and was quite smug about his youthfulness. "Yep, I'd say I'm reaching my singing prime right now. I've got a whole career in front of me."

Darren scoffed. "I thought country singers were all old people. That Willie Nelson looks like my grandad."

The musician stared down at his heavy metal t-shirt and frowned. "It seems your knowledge of the genre is quite limited."

"I know enough," Darren muttered. He hadn't exactly been converted after the performance from the night before.

"I hear that you're going through something of a re-brand," said Nesta, trying to change the subject. "The Golden Wanderers... has a crispy ring to it."

Noel's face lit up. "Yeah, that was a great idea. I think it's going to be big."

"What was Dale's thoughts on that idea?"

There was a short silence, and Noel struggled to hide his surprise. "Dale? He had nothing to do with it. The guy was on the way out anyway. He was stuck in the past. You know he didn't even write his own songs?"

"Really?" Nesta asked, genuinely shocked.

"All his songs were written by some unknown hack," Noel continued. "And he just regurgitated the same ones for years. He's had the same set list forever. I guess the person who wrote those songs must have bitten the dust, too."

Nesta was finding the revelation about Dale's back catalogue of songs quite difficult to accept. One of Dale's early appeals when she first listened to those hits on her husband's CD player was the assumption that he sang from the heart. His lyrics were practically stories from a life of love and heartbreak. Surely, they were not written by someone else.

"So I take it there was a bit of tension in the band before Dale passed away," she said.

"You can say that again," said Noel. He stretched out his arms in a pair of pyjamas that should have been thrown away a long time ago. "And it wasn't just creative differences with me, either." He pointed towards the second campervan. "Stew even got into a fistfight with him not that long ago."

"The drummer?"

"Yeah!" Noel chuckled. "You don't go getting in a fight with a guy who bashes things for a living. Those drummers can be hard as nails. Throw in a temper like Stew's and you're asking for trouble."

Nesta had noticed a certain intensity in the drummer's demeanour when he came to collect his breakfast. There was a wildness in him that even she wouldn't want to test. "What were they fighting over?"

Noel yawned. "What two guys usually fight about — a woman."

Darren was peering through one of the windows in complete fascination. "You guys really live in these things?"

The musician saw the younger man's genuine curiosity and was willing to disregard his initial dislike of the teenager. "Sure we do!" He wandered over to the second campervan and swung open the door. "Wanna take a look?"

"Hey!" a voice cried from inside.

Noel ignored his bandmate's protest. "Get yourself in there and try her out. It's real cosy."

Nesta was quite concerned about Darren contracting some sort of strange disease and didn't want to be held responsible for him catching something. "Don't touch anything!" she called out.

The conditions inside the campervan were as bad as Nesta had feared, and she could smell something rotten as soon as she poked her head inside.

"Sorry about that," said Stew, as she scrunched up her nose. He pointed down at the limited floor space, which was covered in washing. "There's an old takeaway down there somewhere. We're still trying to find it."

Darren had already made himself at home in the empty second bed and lay back with a smile. He could imagine himself as a travelling musician: no responsibilities, no teachers, no concerns. "Where are all your instruments?"

"We keep them in the trailer," Stew muttered, as he plonked his face back down against the pillow. "You wouldn't want a whole drumkit in here."

Nesta looked around at the cluttered environment and could now see why Dale chose to stay up at the guesthouse. "And how do you feel about the change in direction?" she asked.

Stew raised his head up to check who she was talking to. "Who, me?" He sniggered. "Nobody ever asks *my* opinion. The only time a person ever notices a drummer is when he misses a beat. And I never miss a beat!"

"You ever play in any rock bands?" asked Darren, turning to him as though he were at a sleepover.

Stew shook his head. "Where I grew up, kid — in Tennessee — it was all country. Good job, too. I only have the energy these days for a steady rhythm."

"So you're not annoyed about the name change?" asked Nesta.

"Call us what you want!" The drummer placed his arms behind the back of his head. "As long as I'm getting paid."

"Would Dale have had a problem?"

Stew scoffed. "Dale had a problem with everything! The guy was never happy."

"I hear that you and him didn't always get along." Nesta waited for the response and was beginning to feel like she had probed this hothead a little too much.

"He was just selfish! It was either his way or the highway. There was no loyalty there."

Nesta checked to see if his lead guitarist was within earshot and was pleased to find that he had returned to his own camper-van. "But there is with Noel?"

Stew chuckled. "I may be an old drummer, but I ain't stupid. I wasn't born yesterday. Everybody's out for themselves in this business. He's damn talented, don't get me wrong. The guy can play, and he can write songs, but it's just like Dolly used to say — *we boys are just a step on the boss man's ladder*. But I can live with that. Some of us never wanted to climb that stupid ladder in the first place. And, besides — I don't like heights!"

CHAPTER 12

Nesta and Darren made their way along Marine Parade, a road which would take them back towards the sands of Barmouth Beach. It was a walk that highlighted the vast amount of seafront hotels on offer in this popular tourist town, and Darren was beginning to wonder what Nesta had been thinking when booking their current accommodation.

"Look at that one," he said, as they walked past a four-storey hotel. "It's right next to the beach."

"I thought you hated the beach," said Nesta.

Darren sighed. He hated the hills even more and preferred a host that wasn't a raving lunatic. "Does he ever get tired?"

They looked down at the excited Jack Russel, tugging away on his lead.

Nesta shook her head. "We'll need to walk a lot more than this to slow Hari down."

So far, since arriving in Barmouth, they had done more steps than the teenager ever thought was possible in just a couple of days. Surely, he thought, a person's feet could only take so much.

"You've been very quiet," he said.

"Who — me?" Nesta had never been accused of being "quiet" before, but the teenager might have had a point. She had barely said a word since leaving the two campervans parked up behind *The Craig Tavern*. "I just can't believe that Dale didn't write his own songs. It can't be true."

"What difference does that make?" Darren asked. "They're just songs. Who cares who wrote them?"

"His songs were different. They were all personal. We're not talking about a nineties pop group here. Country music is all about soul and storytelling. The two just can't be separated. I just can't get my head around the whole thing."

Darren shrugged. "Doesn't bother me. A good song is a good song. Doesn't matter where it came from. People don't seem to have a problem singing *Jingle Bells* every year."

Nesta was still not convinced. The revelation about Dale Benham's songwriting (or lack there of it) had only highlighted the fact that she really didn't know this man at all. And if they were ever going to get to the bottom of why someone wanted to kill him, she needed to understand who they were dealing with.

"That Noel guy didn't seem to have any trouble jumping in the man's grave," said Darren.

"He certainly did not," said Nesta. "I think we can be confident of one thing — Dale didn't have many people around watching his back. The music industry seems like a lonely business."

They continued along the promenade and came across a woman with enormous sunglasses walking her schnauzer.

Darren squinted. "Isn't that —"

"Yes," said Nesta. "I think it is."

Nia Llywelyn, *The Barmouth Country And Western Festival*'s honorary director, walked as though she were being photographed by a hoard of paparazzi photographers. The only problem was that nobody knew who she was (except for the two people fast approaching her).

The sight of Hari caused the determined schnauzer to start barking, and, unlike the previous encounter with the large German Shepherd, the Jack Russell was quite confident that he had met a worthy opponent this time.

"Hari!" Nesta cried, as he began returning the other dog's growls.

"Willie! Willie, stop it!"

Darren sniggered at the name (inspired by the country legend from Texas).

"I'm so sorry," said Nia. "He's in a right funny mood today."

Nesta crouched down and tickled the schnauzer behind his ears, causing her own dog to get very jealous. "He's adorable," she said. "I'm also quite partial to a bit of Willie Nelson. They even have similar beards."

Darren was no longer amused and stared at the two women laughing.

"You're a country fan?" Nia asked. "You should come along to my festival!"

"Oh," said Nesta. "We already have. In fact, we were there last night."

Nia's face dropped. "You *were*?" She hung her head in shame. "Oh, I'm so sorry. Last night was a complete disaster. Please don't let that put you off coming again."

"The couple at the start seemed okay."

"Julie and Simon?" Nia sighed. "Those old hippies have been regulars at this festival for decades. They're probably the last reliable acts we've got." Her face darkened. "The likes of Nick Franklin are going to ruin my reputation forever."

"I thought he was supposed to be a famous country singer," said Darren. "He told me himself."

Nia howled with laughter. "I'll bet he did! What did he call himself? Country prince of the North West or some rubbish like that?"

"Something like that," an embarrassed Darren muttered. The man had seemed like the real deal when they first met up at the guesthouse. Perhaps it was just the cowboy hat and boots that had fooled him.

"Don't get me wrong," said Nia. "Nick Franklin was hyped to be the next-big-thing in country music when he first came on the scene. He won Best Newcomer and Future Star awards at this very festival on his first year. But things soon went downhill. The guy just couldn't hack it. He even went out to America to cut his teeth in Nashville. But they must have smashed those pearly whites to pieces. He came back a broken man, and his confidence was never the same."

"Is that why he drank so much last night?" asked Nesta. "To calm his nerves?"

Nia nodded. "Although, there's calming your nerves, and then there's obliterating them. I don't think Nick can tell the difference. It's rather sad, I suppose — if it wasn't my festival!"

"I hear you took it over from your father," said Nesta.

Nia was caught off guard by this stranger's knowledge. People didn't normally take such an interest in her little festival these days, especially in its history. "Why, yes. Where did you hear that?"

Nesta smiled. "I was talking to Nick's manager last night at the bar."

"Ah," said Nia with a groan. "The bar is definitely a place you'll find *that* horrid man. I bet he also blamed me for the festival's obvious downfall."

Her remark made Nesta rather uncomfortable, and she was forced to clear her throat. "Oh, he only had good things to say."

"Pah!" Nia roared with laughter. "I don't believe that for one second. That slimy little weasel needs to go get a proper job."

She saw the other two's surprised faces. "As you might be able to tell, I'm not a big fan of agents or managers. They're just a bunch of talentless leeches who sponge off creatives for their own financial gain. It's a seedy career path. Unfortunately for me, I've had to deal with plenty of Robin's sort over the years. And that man is no different." She pulled out a packet of mints and popped a couple in her mouth whilst she was talking. "Now, as for musicians, that's a whole different kettle of fish. I've got plenty of respect for them. It's not easy trying to make a living from making music. Even the best have struggled. You can spend thousands of hours learning an instrument, and it still doesn't guarantee you a career. I mean, if you studied that much doing an engineering degree and couldn't get a paying job, you'd be asking for your money back." Nia continued sucking on her mint and let out a proud smile. "I'm learning an instrument myself, you know. Never played a thing until last year. But it's never too late to try something new."

"Absolutely!" Nesta's face lit up. She had been planning on learning a musical instrument herself now that she had the time. Her one regret in life was that she had given up the piano after one lesson. Granted, she was only twelve at the time, but it was surprising how much those small decisions in life still haunted a person. "What instrument are you learning?"

"The piano," said Nia.

"Are you really?"

Darren let out a yawn, as he prepared to be bored for the next five minutes. If he had to hear about the piano lessons one more time, he was going to sign Nesta up himself.

"It's the best thing I've ever done," Nia continued. "I've been involved in music all my life, but I've always had this slight shame about not being able to play an instrument. My father, who founded this festival, was a magnificent guitar player, and I always loved the idea of being able to join in with a jam. I have my grandmother's old piano gathering dust in the living room. She didn't play herself and would have given anything to see it being used. As fate would have it, I bumped into a local piano teacher who lives up in the hills." She pointed in the direction of Old Barmouth, and the location of a certain guesthouse. Nesta and Darren didn't even need to look at each other on this occasion. There could only be so many piano teachers in that part of town.

"Have you found this teacher useful?" Nesta asked.

"Oh, yes. We've become rather good friends, actually. She's a big supporter of the festival and loves her country music. I stayed clear of her for years, you see." Nia lowered her voice despite there being no chance of being overheard from this distance. "She had a reputation for being a bit obsessive with some of the acts. A proper fruit cake, some might say."

This time, Nesta and Darren couldn't resist a concerned glance at each other.

"Does she live up at Bryn Lodge?" Nesta asked.

"Yes! That's the place!" Nia studied these strangers again. "And there was me thinking you two were tourists."

"We are," said Darren. "Only without any of the fun."

Nesta threw him a disapproving frown. "We tend to get around quite a bit when we visit places. Bryn Lodge is where we're staying."

Nia nodded. "Ah, that makes sense. So, anyway, when I found out that Anwen was a piano teacher, I exchanged a festival pass with some lessons. And now we've become good friends."

Nesta was trying to process this new connection and what it might mean (if it meant anything at all). Such coincidences were normally a cause for concern when it came to murder investigations, as a true coincidence was always highly unlikely.

"She was a big fan of Dale," Nesta said, eventually.

"You can say that again," said Nia. "I think the word is super-fan, these days."

"And what was your opinion of him?"

"Dale?" Nia let out a heavy sigh. "I actually had a lot of respect for the man. He was one of the old school types, you know? He was very loyal. I remember when he was just a warm-up act. It was the good old days when we'd get some of the big names rolling into town. I was a little girl back then, but I remember it like it was yesterday. Dale used to call me Little Lady and share his American sweets." Her face was clouded with nostalgia, as she pictured the sold-out shows of yesteryear. "You could barely get a ticket back then. In the years since I took over, Dale became our biggest star. But we still struggle to fill the seats. I tried to get Ryan Kirby this year."

Darren sniggered. "*The* Ryan Kirby?"

Both women turned to look at the teenager.

"How do you know who that is?" asked Nesta, who hadn't the foggiest.

"He's massive on *TikTok*," Darren muttered. "Even I know who *that* guy is. And I don't even like country."

"Yet," Nia corrected him. "We'll soon change that."

"That's what I keep telling him," said Nesta with a wink.

"Why would Ryan Kirby ever want to play at *this* festival?" Darren asked.

"Good question," Nia snapped. She was clearly still irritated. "His agent turned me down."

"Oh," said Darren, feeling rather bad.

"Dale had once helped the young man get his big break. He referred Ryan to a record producer he once knew. He thought the man owed him one. I guess he thought wrong." Nia shook her head. "It's a chicken and the egg problem — stars want big audiences, but the audiences want to see big stars. You can only do so much."

Nesta nodded. "I can see your problem. What about that young singer who used to be Dale's backing guitarist? He surely has a chance to bring in fresh blood."

"Noel?" Nia looked like she was going to gag. "I'm not a fan. But, then again, I'm just a stubborn, old-fashioned country fan. What do I know?"

"Fair enough," said Nesta with a sigh. She was about to separate Hari from his new friend, as the two dogs were now happily sniffing each other, when she decided to ask the woman one last question: "Any ideas if someone might have wanted Dale dead?"

Nia stared at her. She had not expected *that* question but contemplated it regardless. "Dead is such a strong word. Not everyone liked him, I know that. I despise that manager of his, but it doesn't mean you'll find his body on Barmouth Bridge tomorrow morning."

Nesta thought about the supposed "fist fight" between Dale and his drummer. "I hear he might have had a love affair with someone local."

The festival director smiled. "You really *do* know all the gossip."

"I like to chat with people," said Nesta with an innocent tone in her voice.

"It's true," said Darren. "She likes to chat a lot."

Nesta resisted the urge to scold the young man and tried to remain focused on the conversation. "So, is it true?"

"It was more than just a love affair," said Nia. She almost seemed a little sad. "He used to be in a long term relationship with Susan Tapscott. She owns a gallery on the high street. Lovely woman. Very artistic herself. They were together for years. As time went on, and with Dale having to tour all the time, Susan ended up finding another man. It broke his heart. I honestly believe it's the reason he kept coming back to this town. Susan was the love of his life. He must have been hoping that they still had a chance. Then, eventually, Susan and her husband separated. Dale came back to find out that she was single again."

Nesta listened intently and found the whole story slightly moving. She knew that certain feelings lasted a lifetime, even towards the people who were not meant to be. "Did they get back together?"

Nia checked her watch. "You'd have to ask her about that. I'm not one to get involved in other people's business too much. I hate to gossip."

Darren gave her a cynical frown. "Yes, we can see that."

"Anyway," said Nia, "do come along to some more events, especially our big one at the end of the week."

Nesta nodded. "*The Mountain Theatre*, isn't it?"

Nia clapped her hands. "It's going to be a big night. I'm still working on Ryan Kirby. He would make a great main event."

"Good luck with that," Darren muttered, as the woman and her schnauzer walked away.

He and Nesta continued their walk along the promenade, and the teenager caught sight of the amusement arcades again. "So, what's the plan for today?"

Nesta checked her watch and was glad to see that it was still early. "We'll nip back to the guesthouse and grab the car."

"The car?" Darren stopped walking. "Where are we going?"

"Don't you worry about that. I've got a little surprise for you."

The teenager did not like her giddy expression one bit, and, when it came to Nesta Griffiths, he hated surprises even more.

CHAPTER 13

Kris Neville had his dirty work boots planted firmly on the table when Nesta entered the communal kitchen at Bryn Lodge. The owner's son was busy enjoying his third tea break of the day and sat back in his chair with a local newspaper open.

Nesta had popped in for a cup of tea herself and noticed the man's stained clothes. "You must be Kris."

Kris turned over a page without even taking his eyes off the newspaper. "That's me. I see mam's been talking. She must be very proud."

"Oh, I'm sure she is." Nesta began rooting through the cupboards and was disappointed by the lack of biscuits. "It's very good of you to do all these jobs on her guesthouse."

"That's me, love." Kris grinned. "I'm good as gold. But don't worry — I still bill her for everything, like. A guy's got to make a living."

"Is this what you do for a living?" Nesta asked, watching the man relaxing with his tea. She also saw where the biscuits had gone.

"I do a bit of everything, me." Kris reached into the biscuit tin on his lap and ate the last custard cream. "Jack of all trades, as they say. That's the benefit of living in a seaside town. There's always plenty of hotels and local businesses that need things fixing."

"You're self-employed?"

"Oh, yeah. I don't do well with people telling me what to do. Never have. That's why I work for myself. Plenty of work around. I just don't have the time." Kris stretched out his arms as if he were ready for a short snooze. "If you got a leaky tap or a dodgy door, I'm your man. I've got some business cards in the van. I think the number's out of date on them, though."

Nesta forced out a polite smile. "I'll be sure to keep you in mind." She began boiling the kettle and trying to read the newspaper from behind Kris' shoulder. The article was clearly about Dale Benham, as she could spot the singer's profile a mile off. Unfortunately, her eyesight wasn't good enough to read the details. "Have they caught whoever killed that poor singer?" she asked.

Kris turned around to find her hovering over his shoulder and almost fell off his chair. "Uh, no. This is more of a tribute to his life. I'm sure mam will want to cut it out." He swiftly turned the page.

"It must have been such a shock when he was staying in your own bed and breakfast."

"Can't say I lost any sleep over it," Kris muttered. "I barely knew the bloke. And I didn't care for his music."

Nesta poured her hot water. "But you must have bumped into him a few times whilst he was staying here?"

"Not if I could help it," said Kris. "He thought he was Elvis Presley, the way he walked around here. Mam didn't help with that. It used to make me sick the way she fussed over him. So he could sing a few tunes —- who cares? It's hardly scoring a hat-trick for Liverpool." He shook his head. "I got no time for a washed-up showbiz guy like him. He should try doing a proper job."

"So you never spoke?"

"He had no time for the likes of me. The guy already had my mam in the palm of his hand. He could probably tell I saw right through him. He'd come and go from this place and not even acknowledge me sometimes. One of the only times he spoke to me was when he needed help with a bike puncture. And it was my bike!"

Nesta stirred her tea and was distracted by the thought of Dale's bicycle (or, as it had turned out, Kris' bicycle).

"Yes," she said eventually. "I heard that Dale was a keen cyclist."

Kris let out a grunt. "That's only because he was probably too cheap to hire a car."

"They apparently found his bicycle the morning after he died."

For the first time since she had entered the kitchen, Kris took his attention away from the newspaper and glared at her. "Yeah, I know. It was my bike, remember? The coppers had a few questions about that. My mam should never have let him borrow the thing. Could have landed me in jail for that."

They both shared an awkward silence. Nesta had not expected such an irritable response, which only intrigued her further. "I visited the farm near where the bike was found yesterday. It was a decent trek. Do you know a farmer called Gethin Moore?"

"Gethin?" Kris smiled. "Yeah, I know him. He went to my school. He's got a bit of a reputation in this town."

"What sort of reputation?"

"The kind you get when you've done time."

Nesta swallowed a mouthful of tea. "He's been to prison?"

Kris nodded and returned to his newspaper. "Don't ask me

why. There's a few rumours flying around. Robberies, grand theft auto, assault… maybe all three. The usual crimes."

"Goodness," said Nesta. She would not have described any of those listed crimes "usual" (at least not in her social circles). "And are they true?"

Kris shrugged. "Don't really care. Me and Gethin always got along alright. We've shared a few beers. Seems like an okay bloke. I guess some people get unlucky."

"You mean they get caught," Nesta snapped.

The man laughed. "Yeah, I suppose that's true. He's always been a bit dodgy, Gethin. He doesn't care what people think. Doesn't have to. He lives in the middle of nowhere. He's a bit of a ladies man, too, and I'm not talking about the sheep."

"Any ideas why Dale Benham would be heading in the direction of his farm late at night?"

"God knows," said Kris. "I'm not his mother."

"Speaking of mothers…" Nesta stared at him. "Your mother brought him a hot drink in bed that night."

Kris laughed. "That sounds about right. Don't tell my dad, or he'll think there was something going on between those two."

"Do you think there was something going on?"

The man was rather disgusted by her question. "I don't really like to think about my mother's love life." He slurped his tea and grimaced. "But she was so infatuated with that man, I wouldn't put anything past her. I'm sure she wouldn't have said no, put it that way."

Now it was Nesta's turn to be disgusted. "Infatuated, you say?" She was surprised that the man even had such a word in his vocabulary. He didn't strike her as a grade-A student.

"It's weird," said Kris. "Dad was always jealous of her obsession with that singer, long before they met. I suppose it's quite normal for your wife to have a crush on a famous person. I had a girlfriend once who fancied the pants off George Clooney. I didn't care. I have a thing for Margot Robbie. But it might be a different story if George Clooney was staying in my house."

Nesta considered his argument and thought he made a good case. It can't have been easy for Richard Neville, having the person that his wife had openly declared her love for in his presence every day. Fantasies were one thing, but befriending a famous person in such a way was not something that happened all the time. Whilst Anwen had made her dream come true in getting to know her lifelong idol, Richard had been very unlucky indeed.

"I don't suppose that Nick Franklin receives the same treatment as Dale?" she asked.

Kris chuckled. "*That* wannabe? Nah. He gets the same service as every other paying guest. Dad had to take him to the surgery this morning. The guy managed to hurt his leg last night."

Nesta had a sudden flashback of Nick falling off the stage. It *had* looked quite painful. "He's broken something?"

Kris shook his head. "I doubt it. Probably just being a big drama queen. I played a whole football match with a broken rib once. He needs to toughen up."

The thought of an injured Nick made Nesta feel quite sorry for him. It was the last thing the singer needed before his big gig. Perhaps, she thought, falling off that stage might literally have been his last big break.

"Here you are," said Darren.

Nesta looked up to see the restless teenager squirming in the doorway. "Are you alright?"

Darren began crossing his legs. "There's an out-of-order sign on the bathroom door!"

Kris looked up from his newspaper. "Oh, yeah. Sorry about that. I'm in the middle of installing a new syphon. Won't be long. Just need to finish this —" He lifted up his mug of tea.

Darren's eyes widened. "Are you serious? I'm bursting!"

Kris sighed. "Alright, fine. Use the bathroom at mam and dad's across the road. They don't lock the front door, so don't bother knocking."

Of all the homes to visit, Anwen Neville's house was far from the top of Darren's list, however, nature was calling, and he headed straight outside in a hurry.

Anwen and Richard Neville's home was visible from *Bryn Lodge*'s front drive, and Darren went running across the public road that separated the two properties.

The front door, as predicted by Kris, was indeed unlocked, and the teenager slipped inside to be confronted with pink walls and a flowery carpet.

His first instinct was to head upstairs, as he heard the high-pitched singing of Anwen Neville coming from the living room. The loud wails were accompanied by her energetic piano play-ing, and Darren snuck his way up the staircase like a weary mouse.

After finding the bathroom, he gave himself a short moment of relief before realising that he had to get back outside again. The last thing he wanted was another awkward conversation with his bizarre host and was prepared to do everything in his power to escape undetected.

As he headed back towards the bannisters, Darren's atten-tion was caught by a view through the nearby window. He ignored the muffled singing and leant across the windowsill to get a better look. Down below was the Neville's back garden, and Richard appeared to be frantically digging a hole in one of his flower beds.

The exhausted man paused for a moment to catch his breath and took a paranoid glance back towards the house. His guilty expression was covered in a layer of sweat, and he returned to his digging with a second wind.

Darren's eyes widened, as he peered down at a wheelbarrow with a mysterious object wrapped in black, plastic material. The shape reminded him of a human torso, and he stepped away from the windowsill to find that the music downstairs had stopped.

All was silent, until a piercing scream caused him to gasp.

CHAPTER 14

Darren could still hear Anwen's scream rattling in his ears hours later. The sight of him on the upstairs landing had caused her to accuse the teenager of "burglary" and "thievery", and Darren had been forced to defend himself like a witch at the stake. After all, it was her own son who had given him permission to enter her home, but that excuse did not fly with a woman who knew a juvenile delinquent when she saw one. She might as well have dragged him out of the house by his earlobe, and, if he was on her watchlist before, the teenager was now under a microscope.

Fortunately, Darren currently had an entire estuary between him and Anwen Neville. Nesta's afternoon "surprise" had finally been revealed, which involved a ride on the *Fairbourne Railway*.

"Here we go!" Nesta cried, as the little steam train blew its whistle. She clapped her hands with delight and gave her grumpy fellow passenger a nudge. "Isn't this fun?"

Darren folded up his arms and watched the scenery begin to move, as he sat beside her in a miniature carriage with a dog's tail wagging against his head. The teenager was still reeling from his encounter with Anwen and grateful that he hadn't been the next one buried in the flowerbed.

"He could have been burying anything," said Nesta once they were chugging along at a steady rate.

"Exactly," said Darren. "It could have been *anything*."

Nesta began waving at the passing pedestrians on the main road. "Well, this should take your mind off the Nevilles for a bit. Wait until you see the view at the other end."

"I can't wait," Darren muttered.

"You can probably get some nice footage of the train for the video channel."

Darren turned to look at her. "What's a tiny steam train got to do with true crime?"

"It'll look great on camera," said Nesta. "I'm sure the viewers would like to see it."

"We don't work for the tourism board," Darren snapped. "The people who watch our channel want to hear about real life murder investigations. Not how nice the attractions are in Fairbourne."

Nesta shook her head. "I think you'd be surprised. You've seen it yourself. Remember that comment one of the viewers made recently? She said that she came for the crime but came back for the investigators. That's you and me! I'd say the viewers are as interested in what we do as the crimes."

Darren let the idea sink in. He couldn't help but be flattered by the idea of people taking an interest in him. That certainly was not the case in school or real life in general. He had never been popular amongst his peers, and it was nice to know that there were people out there who didn't just ignore him. But he also knew the ways of the internet a lot better than Nesta did. One comment did not reflect the opinion of a whole community, and true crime fans needed their fix of theories and evidence. A little segment on the *Fairbourne Railway* was not going to cut it for the majority of people, and, if they were going to keep their legion of loyal followers, they needed to please the majority.

Darren also knew that the supposed interest in the "investigators" was not in him alone. Without Nesta, his channel would simply not have garnered the interest that it already had. As much as it pained him to admit it to himself, even *he* could not deny that. They had now become an unlikely double act, and you couldn't have one without the other. As much as he owed a lot of his online popularity to this unlikely ally, he was determined to not allow Nesta to hear him admit that.

"I just don't see the big deal in a railway line that lasts for two miles," he said.

"My children used to absolutely adore riding on here," said Nesta. She let out a sad sigh. "So many nice memories. It's good to see that this is still going. Unlike a lot of things these days! The amount of times I visit somewhere and the places are closed down or nonexistent." Her face lit up again. "They even still had the model railway!"

Darren had already been acquainted with the miniature railway system back at the station. Although he was not quite as excited as Nesta (and had been embarrassed by her loud squeal when she discovered it), Darren had secretly enjoyed pressing the button and watching the model come to life. Some things never got old, he had realised.

They both sat back and enjoyed the rest of their short journey towards the estuary. The small locomotive up ahead pulled its line of carriages with relative ease along this scenic route, which included a perfect view of the aforementioned nine-hole golf course.

"There she is," said Nesta, watching a man in shorts swinging his club, only to see his ball disappear into the nearby sand dunes. "We'll have to do some holes later."

Darren chuckled before realising that she was being serious.

"You know," she added, "at the last stop, you're able to take a ferry back to Barmouth. That would be fun, wouldn't it? I've never actually done it."

The teenager turned to her in disbelief. "What about the car?"

Nesta paused. He made a good point. They *had* driven all the way along the Mawddach River and back across the Penmaenpool Toll Bridge — just to get all the way back around to Fairbourne. There had been no shortcuts without investing in a decent rowing boat. "I suppose we can catch the ferry back again."

"No," said Darren, firmly. "No way. There's no way I'm getting on no boat. The train idea was bad enough."

Nesta began sulking for a few minutes, until she saw a black hole approaching them. "Oh! We're about to go under the tunnel!"

Darren's unexcited face disappeared into complete darkness, until they reemerged on the other side of the tunnel.

"The children used to love this bit," said Nesta. She turned to find Darren filming the view through his window and smiled. It was hard not to be impressed, even for him.

Eventually, their train arrived at the final stop. *The Harbour View Café* was situated beside the short platform and Darren breathed a sigh of relief. "Great, there's food. I'm starving."

Nesta waited for the teenager to run inside and grab himself three bags of crisps and a *Coke*. "You know that none of those things count as actual food?" she asked.

Darren gave her a confused look with a mouth full of crisps. "Tastes like food to me."

Nesta rolled her eyes and suggested that they take a little walk to the small beach whilst their train was preparing to turn around. There were at least twenty minutes until their return journey, and Nesta was hoping to catch sight of the ferry.

She was not disappointed, as they caught sight of the small passenger boat making its way back to Penrhyn Point. Over to the right, they could see Barmouth Bridge stretching out across the estuary, which seemed longer now than it had done the day before. Whilst Darren began throwing some sticks for an excited Hari, Nesta couldn't help but notice a figure lurking in the long grass up above. For a moment, she thought the man was trying to talk to her, until it became clear that he was filming himself on a mobile phone.

"Whatever has the world come to?" she muttered and took another look at the panoramic view. Some things, she thought to herself, were best experienced with your own eyes. As she turned around to give this tourist another judgmental scowl, she spotted something on the person's t-shirt.

The man in the grass was dressed in jeans, a cowboy hat and had an image of Johnny Cash across his large stomach.

"You must be in town for the festival," said Nesta, having climbed her way up the steep bank.

Kenny Leith lowered his phone and grinned.

Nesta had half-expected to hear an American accent coming out of his mouth, but, instead, the man spoke like a native Scotsman. "Aye, is it that obvious?" The man tipped his hat and chuckled.

"I didn't mean to interrupt your filming," said Nesta. "I thought there might be a better view from up here."

Kenny saw that she was looking at his phone. "Oh, don't worry about it. I already got a decent take. The audio's terrible in this wind. It probably won't make the Final Cut, anyway."

His use of technical language intrigued Nesta. "You make videos?"

"Oh, aye. I may not look like it, but I'm a fully-fledged online content creator." He saw the confusion in the woman's face. "Basically, I make videos and put them up on the internet."

"Ah, right, I see." Nesta nodded.

"I've even got my own channel," said Kenny with a proud raise of his chin.

"That's brilliant! So have I!"

Now it was Kenny's turn to look confused. "You have your own streaming channel?"

"Why, yes! It's got lots of viewers, and we're growing all the time." Nesta turned around and pointed at Darren, who was busy filming at the water's edge. "In fact, there's my cameraman over there."

A dumbfounded Kenny, who did not have his own camera operator, didn't know what to say. "Oh, well, that's great. What's the theme of your channel?"

"Murder," said Nesta, before realising that she had uttered a rather morbid word for a casual conversation. "Or I should say — true crime. My friend and I cover local crimes, and we try to solve them as best we can. Although, we tend to be moving further afield as of late. Bala only has so many interesting crimes taking place."

From one content creator to the next, Kenny was genuinely intrigued. "Is that right?"

"And what is the subject of *your* online videos?" Nesta asked, as though it were a question she asked everyday.

Kenny almost seemed embarrassed to admit it. "It's mainly about me — Kenny Leith." He let out a cough. "But the topic I mainly talk about is country music. I like to travel all over the country — and America, too, when I can — covering artists and music events."

"How exciting," said Nesta. "And how many viewers do you have? Not that anyone's counting!" She giggled. "Although, there is *literally* a counter beside the video, which I've never liked."

"I average a hundred views per video," said Kenny.

"Goodness." Nesta tried to hide her disappointment. Had

someone told her a year ago that a hundred people had watched their video on the internet, she would have asked for an autograph. "Good for you."

"Yeah, well. I've got a very loyal fanbase. And, like me, they love their country music. I'm planning a trip to Nashville next year which the viewers will go nuts for."

"I can only imagine," said Nesta. "Have you enjoyed the festival so far? You must have been at the event last night at the pub. I thought I might have seen you there." Now that she thought about it, she *did* remember seeing a man in the audience with a cowboy hat and boots (but that was to be expected at a country and western festival).

"I was there," said Kenny. "Shame about the last act. I'd heard good things about Nick Franklin." He let out a sly grin. "Although, I did manage to get some footage of the stage fall. That's the sort of stuff that goes viral."

Nesta frowned. She hated the idea of someone taking pleasure in another person's misfortune — let alone posting it on the internet for the world to see. It struck her as very cruel. "They say he might have broken something." She waited for a guilty look, but it never came. "Did you get much footage of Dale Benham?"

Kenny's eyes sparkled. "Are you kidding? You bet I did." He tensed his body with excitement and jiggled his phone. "I've got hours of footage on this thing."

Nesta was suddenly a little excited herself. Perhaps this train journey on the *Fairbourne Railway* was proving more useful than Darren realised. "Have you shared any of it yet?"

Nick shook his head. "I'm going to compile it all together when I get home. This stuff is pure gold. Do you know how much broadcasters and documentary makers can pay for footage of a dead artist? I have the last few days of Dale Benham's life captured on video. Nobody else can say that."

"You must be very happy," said Nesta. She looked at the man as though he were a giant vulture in a cowboy hat. "How did you get so much footage?"

Kenny leant towards her with a mischievous smile, and she could smell his poor hygiene. "Let's just say that I bought him a lot of drinks. If there's one way to a country singer's heart, it's whiskey. He was quite happy for me to film as much as I liked — so long as I kept the drinks coming."

Nesta nodded. If there was one thing she had learnt about the late Dale Benham so far, it was that he loved anything for free. "Sounds like you hit the jackpot." She stared at the man's phone and prepared to flutter her eyelashes. "Any chance I could get a little peek?"

CHAPTER 15

"Sounds like a right weirdo to me," said Darren, as he filmed a close-up of his golf ball.

When it came to describing Kenny Leith (the self-proclaimed "videographer"), Nesta would have chosen a slightly different word to "weirdo", but she agreed that he was a rather strange man. "The lengths people will go to for their online content is astounding," she said.

"Yep." Darren grabbed a quick shot of the surrounding golf course. "Anyone who goes around filming videos about dead people needs to get their heads tested. Some people need to get a life."

Nesta agreed. It was very distasteful. "He supposedly has a lot of footage of Dale, too." She had failed in her little pursuit to secure a private screening of Kenny's videos and imagined that watching footage of a man who was days away from the end of his life would have been incredibly harrowing.

"Why didn't he show it to you?" Darren asked.

"Some rubbish about exclusivity rights and non-disclosure agreements," said Nesta. "You would think the man had CCTV footage from the Watergate scandal on his phone. He said it was mainly drunken rants from Dale, and an impromptu gig down at the harbour. Ideally, I would have liked to have watched the videos. You never know what you might find." She looked over to find Darren watching something on his own phone. "Are you even listening?"

The teenager chuckled and showed her his screen. "Is this your man?"

Nesta stared at a video of Kenny Leith talking to camera whilst he travelled on a small boat. "Wait a minute..." She frowned at the man, as he began singing. "Isn't that the Barmouth Ferry?" A confused Nesta looked up in the direction of the estuary, which she could still see over in the distance beyond the golf course. "How is that possible? I can see Penrhyn Point behind him in the video. Has he taken this ferry twice?"

Darren shook his head and pointed to his phone. "This is a live video."

"What?" Nesta could not believe what she was hearing. "You're telling me that the man is recording this video as we speak? Right over there?"

They both turned to the direction of the estuary.

"Yep," said Darren. "And the content is pretty shocking. It's just a man, waffling away on a boat. No wonder he's hardly got any subscribers."

Nesta shook her head. "Right, then." She lifted up her golf ball and scoring card. "Let's focus on the task in hand, shall we?"

Darren sighed and began swinging his golf club around like a samurai sword. He knew this would embarrass his golfing partner and had warned her that a round of golf was a bad idea. Firstly, he had no idea how to play, and, secondly, he was fairly certain that Nesta didn't have a clue either. And, so, he prepared for the blind to start leading the blind in a game he didn't even see the point of.

"It's fairly straight forward," said Nesta, trying to scope out their first flag. "You just need to get the ball in the hole by making as few hits as you can."

"I sort of gathered that," Darren grumbled. "So what's all that stuff about birdies and over pars?"

Nesta looked at him as if it was an utterly stupid question but was struggling to come up with an answer. "Never mind about that. Just stop talking and give that thing a good swing."

Darren placed his ball down and prepared to strike it as hard as he could. He didn't care much for golf but relished the idea of whacking something with brute force.

Nesta took several steps back and watched the teenager make his first shot. After narrowly missing his ball, a furious Darren continued to make another three failed attempts. Trying to catch his breath, he heard a giggle coming from Nesta's direction and decided that five times would be a charm. With his strongest swing yet, the ball went soaring through the air, and he let out a victorious cry.

They both watched the golf ball go flying off into the distance, only to then land in a patch of long grass at the edge of the course.

Nesta began tutting, as a disappointed Darren closed his eyes in despair. "Oh, dear," she said. "You're going to need a decent pitching wedge to get it out of there. Right, my turn!" She stepped forward like a seasoned golfer and sent her own ball straight in the direction of the first hole. "Did I make the green? Goodness, I'm better than I thought. I guess golf isn't as hard as it looks."

Darren watched her go strutting off towards the green and wished he had stayed behind in the car with Hari. A couple of holes later, and the young man was at his wits end.

"Are we really still only on the third hole?" he asked, using a nine-iron to prop himself up. "This is going to take forever!" Had he known how much walking would be involved, he would have suggested going back to the guesthouse (which, considering his relationship with the owners, was really saying something).

Nesta ignored his complaining and remained focused on her putting. She gave the golf ball a gentle knock and sent it rolling into the open hole. "Golf is not about getting to the last hole," she said. "It's about enjoying the journey." Nesta straightened her back and pointed towards the building on the other side of the course. "Or there wouldn't be a course full of holes at all. Everyone would just be gathered in the clubhouse putting their feet up."

"Sounds good to me," Darren muttered. He saw her scribbling in her precious score card. "Why do you even bother keeping the scores? It's clear who's winning!" The teenager pointed towards a pit of sand. "I've lost half of my balls, and I gave up trying to get the last one out of there."

"It's not *just* about beating each other," said Nesta, putting extra emphasis on the word "just". "Golf is about self-improvement. We're playing against ourselves as much as we are against an opponent. Like a crossword puzzle or... yoga."

"Yoga?!" Darren shook his head. "I'd hardly compare standing in the middle of a field full of holes to *stretching*."

Nesta took a deep breath and tried to remain patient. "I'm talking about improving your personal best. It's like learning anything — the more you study and practise, the better you get. That's why you hear golfers talk about their individual handicaps — not about how many games they've won."

Darren was still not convinced. "You lost me at the word *studying*. Don't start bringing school into it. Besides, how come you know so much about golf, all of a sudden?"

Nesta picked her ball up and shrugged. "I'm learning as I go. But I can see the appeal of it."

"Sure," Darren muttered. "When you're winning..."

"Right," said Nesta, crossing off her scoresheet and searching for the next hole. "Three down, six to go."

As Nesta scanned the rest of the course, her squinted eyes stumbled upon a figure on the fifth hole. "Look who it is," she said.

Darren turned to see that the man lining up his final shot was none other than Gethin Moore. The farmer was dressed in formal golfing attire and appeared to be taking his game quite seriously. "Wow," said Darren. "I hardly recognised him without the Wellington boots. He must have a lot of time on his hands." Realising that Nesta had already made a b-line to the fifth hole, he began wheeling their rented golf clubs like a reluctant caddy.

"Fancy seeing you here," said Nesta.

Gethin watched his golf ball go rolling past the hole and let out a grunt. He stood up to find the same woman who had been standing in his yard only a day before. "Are you following me?"

Nesta gave him an innocent gasp. "Why, not at all. As luck would have it, we were enjoying a nice round of golf and there you are."

"Luck?" asked Gethin, who was still annoyed by his last shot. "I'd say you've brought none of that."

"Ah," said Nesta, noticing his ball on the green beneath her feet. "You might need to keep your back straighter. I find that helps."

The farmer scoffed. "You play *golf* now?"

"It would appear so." Nesta twirled her golf club. "Turns out I'm a bit of a natural, actually. Who knew?"

"Good for you," Gethin muttered and began re-positioning himself for another shot. "Now, if you don't mind, I'm sort of in the middle of something."

Nesta watched him take another swing and listened to the

sweet, gentle sound of a golf ball landing in a hole. "You see! I knew you'd make it in the end."

Gethin squeezed the handle of his club and refused to get upset. "I appreciate the support. But I'm not really used to spectators." He began walking to his next hole and was surprised that this woman was not taking a hint.

"I'm sure you're not," said Nesta strolling beside him whilst trying to keep up with his brisk pace. "In fact, it's probably quite a lonely existence living out here."

"I like it," said Gethin. "Being alone is actually how I prefer it."

"Now I know people *say* that. But it can't be easy. I live alone myself, actually."

"Do you?" Gethin asked, pretending to be surprised. "How unexpected."

"Yes, I know." Nesta maintained his pace, until they reached the next starting point. "There's nothing wrong with it. I've grown to be okay with it myself. But it's good to have someone to talk to."

Gethin prepared to take his own shot and wondered if this woman would ever give up. "I can see you're a fan of talking. But I'm not the sociable type."

"That's not what I hear," said Nesta.

The farmer froze halfway through his shot. He put his next swing on hold and turned to her with a frown. "What do you mean by that?"

Nesta saw the concern in his face and smiled. "I was talking to one of your friends this morning. Kris Neville?"

Gething laughed. "Pah! You think Kris Neville is a friend of mine? He's a waste of space. Always has been."

"You were in school together," said Nesta. "He made out that you're a bit of a ladies man."

The farmer was happy to be flattered. "Only compared to

him. I don't think any girl would want to touch Kris Neville with a barge pole. He looks like he hasn't washed in weeks."

Nesta stepped back and admired his golfing clothes. "Where as you, Mr Moore, appear to have quite the dress sense for a man who farms for a living."

Once again, Gethin accepted her compliment with a smug nod. The golfing clothes had not been cheap. "I have other streams of income other than farming. You got to have your fingers in lots of pies these days."

"Is that right?" asked Nesta. "Are we talking about other businesses?"

"We're *talking* far too much," said Gethin. He bent over and took his shot.

They both watched the ball sail across the course and land perfectly on the smooth putting surface of the sixth hole.

"Very nice," said Nesta. "You certainly play golf like a businessman."

Gethin sniggered. "Maybe my luck is changing."

Nesta stared at his confident smile and tried to read between the lines. "Considering the two of you are not friends," she said, "Kris seemed to know a lot about you. It sounds like you've not always been so lucky when it comes to the law."

"Here we go," said Gethin. "Is this about my stint inside?" He saw her curious stare and nodded. "I bet he told you I robbed a post office or something. People jump to all kinds of conclusions in this town."

Nesta shook her head. "I can't imagine your crime was too serious, or you wouldn't be here playing a round of golf."

The farmer smiled. "You're obviously smarter than all the gossipers around here. You'd think I'd killed someone the way they treat me."

"You don't have to have been to prison to kill anyone," said Nesta.

Gethin went silent and stared at her to check if she was being serious. Once he had made his mind up, the man let out a laugh. "You remind me of my mam. If I didn't know any better, I'd say you were a copper in a previous career. Now, funnily enough, I don't normally like coppers, but I quite liked my mam."

"You're close," snapped Nesta. He was beginning to annoy her now. She knew trouble when she saw it, and Gethin Moore was more trouble than a broken-down car. "My husband was a police officer."

"Ah," said Gethin with a nod. "I knew there was a faint smell of bacon in the air."

Nesta squeezed the golf club in her hand and pictured herself whacking the man over the head with it. Surely, she thought, *that* would have been a hole in one. Instead of acting on her wildest fantasy, she took a long, deep breath and calmed herself down. If there was anyone not worth going to jail for, it was *this* man. "Did I tell you I grew up on a farm?"

Gethin shook his head with disinterest.

"My father always used to have a saying," Nesta continued.

"Let me guess," said Gethin with a sigh. "Red sky at night, shepherd's delight?"

Nesta let out a pretend laugh. "Clever, but no." She lifted up her club and prepared to walk away. "He used to say that you could always judge a farmer by his livestock."

"Did he really?" Gethin let out a smug grin. "And what did you make of my sheep?"

There was a long pause whilst Nesta considered her answer.

"Small," she said.

"Small?"

"Small. Very small."

A confused Gethin watched the woman walk off across the green.

CHAPTER 16

"What did you expect?" Darren asked. "We already know the guy's a criminal." He began stroking Hari's head, as the Jack Russell curled up in the footwell.

Nesta clutched the steering wheel and shook her head. "It doesn't mean he had to be so rude." She pictured that egotistical farmer in his golfing attire. He reminded her of a grapefruit — appealing on the outside, sour on the inside.

They were now making the return journey back to Barmouth on a road so long and winding that it made Darren want to heave. He had suffered terrible car sickness as a child, and it seemed that Nesta's driving was bringing it all back up again.

"Surely," he said, once they had crossed the Afon Mawddach for the second time that day, "there must be a quicker way back than having to go all the way around like this. It should only take us twenty minutes. It's probably quicker to walk."

"Maybe you should have flown back on that drone of yours," said Nesta, who was rather enjoying the scenic route.

By the time they had driven all the way back up to Bryn

Lodge, Darren had fallen asleep. When he slowly opened his eyes, the teenager was horrified to see Anwen Neville's face looking down on him. "For the love of —" Darren began trying to crawl back into his car seat, as the woman continued to stare at him through the windscreen.

"Did you have a good day out?" Anwen asked, as Nesta approached her on the outside of the vehicle.

"It was a wonderful trip down memory lane," Nesta said, stretching out her arms to recover from the drive. "I do love Fairbourne." She noticed that Anwen was dressed in a formal suit that didn't look like it saw the light of day very often. "You look very smart."

Anwen blushed and fixed her hair. "We're off for our monthly date night," she said, whilst checking her watch and glancing back at the house. "Although, if my husband takes any longer, we'll lose our table."

"How lovely," said Nesta. "Are you going anywhere nice?"

"There's a fish restaurant down by the harbour. We haven't been there since our wedding anniversary. They do some really good cheap deals before six o'clock. But if that slow coach takes any longer, we'll be paying full price."

A long term marriage really was priceless, Nesta thought to herself, and the Nevilles were living proof. "Well, I hope you both enjoy your meal. Will you be out all evening?"

"We usually go for a couple of drinks afterwards at one of the local pubs," said Anwen. "You have to treat yourself once in a while. You know, keep the romance alive." She turned around and screamed: "Richard!! What on earth are you doing in there?! You're making us late!"

Her flustered husband came stumbling out the front door whilst still doing up his old suit jacket. "I told you I was coming!" he cried.

The couple bickered their way to the car parked across the road and drove off for their night out.

Darren had waited to make sure that the vehicle had disappeared out of sight before making his way out of Nesta's car with Hari. "I thought they were never going to leave." He turned to see that Nesta was deep in thought and didn't like the mischievous look on her face. "What? What is it?"

Nesta looked up towards one of the windows on the first floor. "They're apparently out all evening."

The teenager waited for her to elaborate but feared what she was about to suggest. "That's good," he said. "That means we can just chill." The silence was killing him. "Right?"

"We've been meaning to have a proper look at Dale's room," said Nesta with a smile. "No time like the present."

Darren groaned. "Please, no. Not that. It's been a long day."

"Just a quick peek."

"What if they come back?"

DARREN DIDN'T GET his question answered, and, before he knew it, they were both standing outside Dale Benham's former room. Nesta was fairly certain that the door was left unlocked, and she wasn't disappointed.

"Are you not coming in?" she asked.

Darren remained frozen in the doorway. "Maybe I should stay here and keep a lookout."

"Don't be daft!" Nesta grabbed him by the arm and pulled him inside. "Get as much as you can on that camera phone of yours."

"You do realise that *your* phone also has a camera?"

Nesta scoffed. "Like I'm ever going to work out that stupid thing. Come on, start rolling! When else do we get to visit the bedroom of a murder victim? And this one's been left completely intact. It's a gift."

Darren reluctantly pulled out his phone and started filming. "You really are colder than I think sometimes…"

The belongings of Dale Benham were still scattered around the room. He had certainly been a man who travelled light, with only a couple of small bags and a suitcase on display.

The most notable item was an old guitar case which Nesta had begun caressing with her fingers. She found it hard to believe that this was Dale Benham's actual guitar case within her very own grasp. It would likely become a sought-after collectable, and it pained her to think that it was still in the possession of Anwen Neville. How easy it would have been to stick it in the back of her car for safekeeping, but she knew that Anwen would soon notice it missing.

Before she could finish her quiet moment with what was now, surely, a piece of musical history, the case was snatched away and opened up on the bed.

"Awesome," said Darren, pulling out the guitar with the care of an orangutan. "I've always wanted to try one of these." He flung the instrument over his knee and began plucking at the strings. With a few strums of his hand, the impatient teenager created a noise that made his listener want to cover up her ears. Even Darren was shocked by the unpleasant noise and had hoped to create something on par with an Ed Sheeran song. "I guess this is harder than it looks." He picked up a cowboy hat sitting on the bedside table and placed it on his head. "At least now I look the part!"

Nesta gave him a disapproving frown and snatched the guitar back. "Will you show some respect?! The owner of this guitar was alive and well not so long ago."

Darren began sulking and slowly removed his hat. "That's rich coming from a person who wanted to raid the dead person's room like some gravedigger." He grabbed his phone and went back to filming the room. His tiny lens went hovering over the various belongings like a digital metal detector, until he reached the small desk in the corner of the room.

Folders were scattered across the table, and a framed photograph contained an elderly woman with white hair and a proud posture. Darren's attention was drawn by a map that was scrunched up behind all the clutter. For one thing, he had rarely even come across a physical map (having last seen one in a pirate film) and was used to navigating the world via his mobile phone. When you were used to scrolling across miles of land using the tip of your finger, a paper map seemed clumsy and cumbersome.

"Here we go," he said, addressing his remark to the only person he knew who *did* still use a physical map. "Do you reckon we'll find treasure?"

Nesta finished putting away the guitar with the delicacy of a pastry chef and rushed over to the desk. She watched Darren open up the map, and her eyes widened. "That's Barmouth."

The teenager was surprised by her surprise. "Well, yeah. It's not like I expected Budapest." The map was swiped out of his hands and used to *whack* him on the top of the head. "Alright, clever clogs." Nesta re-opened the map and pointed to the various pencil marks. "That's the area we were walking yesterday."

Darren squinted and began to suspect that all those hours staring at a phone were already starting to impair his eyesight. He recognised the bridge and followed it across the estuary to a vast area of land on the other side. Further up was a dot of black ink which had been specifically marked.

"Isn't that where the farm is?" he asked, pointing at the mark.

Nesta shook her head. "The farm is much further down. This is a completely different spot."

They both stared at the mark as though it were literally an X on a treasure map. "So, what's over at this bit?"

"Your guess is as good as mine," said Nesta with a smile. "But whatever's there must have been of particular interest."

"Maybe we can check it out later on my phone app," said Darren, who was hoping that such a rural area had actually been photographed from the ground.

Nesta tried not to sound too appalled by the idea. "Or," she said, "we can go there ourselves and see the real thing."

Darren scrunched up his forehead. The idea was not appealing, and he did not fancy another long walk any time soon. "It's probably not something to spend too much time on. It might just be an accidental smudge." He pointed to the framed photograph. "Her, on the other hand..."

"Ah, yes." Nesta gazed at the woman staring back at them. "Lydia Benham."

The teenager was very confused. "What? You know that woman?"

Nesta sighed. "It's obviously Dale's mother. Were you paying any attention to what that manager at the pub was saying?"

Darren tried to hide his embarrassment. "I tend to zone out when there's music on."

His comment was ignored and Nesta picked up the photograph. "She was apparently from Barmouth, originally, and she moved to Texas and married some wealthy oil tycoon. As you do!" Nesta was imagining a man like Colonel Parker (or even Colonel Sanders), dressed in a white suit and hat. Her jovial mood saddened at the thought of the conclusion to Lydia's story. "She ended up dying with dementia. Poor thing. Dale must have been heartbroken. He seemed close to her. At least now they can be together again."

Darren was initially confused at her remark, until he realised that she was referring to their reunion in the afterlife. Personally, he didn't have very strong views on what happened to a person after they died. Darren had often compared it to being born, a concept he had heard in a children's film once. Whenever he saw archive footage of a time before he was born, he often imagined that it was the same as being dead. It made the idea of death a lot easier to accept in his mind. After all, he had decided, there had been plenty of years *before* the existence of Darren Price — and *that* hadn't been an unpleasant feeling, whatsoever. According to Darren, Dale Benham was none the wiser that he was dead any more than *he* had been before being born.

"Are you alright?" Nesta asked. The teenager had gone very quiet and appeared to be deep in thought.

Darren snapped back into reality and nodded. "Sorry, I was just thinking about something."

"Anything interesting?" Nesta asked, trying not to sound too doubtful.

"Just death," said Darren, very matter-of-factly.

"Lovely," said Nesta. "I always used to wonder what my students were thinking about when they weren't paying attention. Never mind about death. You'll have plenty of time to think about that later. Now, let's stay focused on the task in hand."

Darren reached out and grabbed a small leather-bound address book underneath one of the folders. "What's this?"

Nesta peered over his shoulder. "That's an address book. It's something people used to use in the old days to store numbers and addresses. You probably have it all kept in the bubble." She began waving her arms in the air like a fortuneteller.

"I know what an address book is," Darren snapped. "Plus, I think you're talking about the *cloud*."

"Come again?"

"It's called the *cloud* — not the bubble."

Nesta shook her head and signalled for him to open up the address book. They glanced over pages of names and addresses, all with American zip codes.

"Stop there," said Nesta.

Darren's fingers paused on a page with a Welsh address. "Llwyngwril," he muttered.

"That's not far from here," said Nesta. "It's a little village on the coastal road. About halfway from here to Tywyn I'd say."

"Danny Cecil," said Darren, looking at the name above the address. "Who could that be?"

"I know Dale had family in this area. Which makes sense, seeing as his mother was from Barmouth." Nesta pointed to his phone. "Might be worth taking a selfie." A confused Darren stared at her. "You know what I mean — a photo, snapshot — whatever you call it."

The teenager shook his head and placed his phone above the address to capture it on his phone. "What about all these folders? I'm not taking photos of all of them."

Nesta picked up a random folder and opened it up. Her hand pulled out a pile of A4 sheets covered in writing. She studied the words and her face lit up. "They're all lyrics."

"Song lyrics?"

"I know this one," said Nesta, showing him the words to a verse. "It's the song 'Butterfly Wings'."

"Sounds like a rubbish name for a song to me," said Darren.

Nesta cleared her throat and, without any warning or permission, began singing one of Dale's greatest hits. "Ohh-hhh... you can't catch a break when you ain't got a gal, but I got me my own sweet little butterfly..."

Darren stared at her in disbelief, as she continued all the way through into the first chorus. "Please stop."

Despite his protests, the singing continued, and he began

rooting through the rest of the folders. He ignored the impromptu line dance going on beside him and found another collection of lyrics and sheet music. He prayed that Nesta was not planning on singing out every single one of these songs, and was about to cry out in protest, when a small photograph slipped out of the folder and into his hand.

The singing stopped, and they both gathered around the image of a small boy standing next to a sailing boat.

"I think we'll maybe hold onto this one," said Nesta, slipping it into her purse. "See if we can work out who this is."

As the two intruders prepared to finish up their little raid, a door *slam* caused them both to freeze.

"That sounded like the front door," said Darren.

Nesta hushed him. "It can't be. That was too close. It must have been the bathroom."

"Let's get out of here!"

"Wait!" Nesta pulled him back and placed a finger across her lips. "We're safer staying in here. Just keep quiet."

They both stared at each other with worried faces, as a series of creaky floorboards increased their heart rates. The thumping sound became louder, until the door handle on the other side of the room began to move.

Darren let out a nervous gasp, and the door to Dale's room flew open.

CHAPTER 17

The door was wide open, and Nick Franklin hobbled into the room on a pair of crutches. The singer's right foot was covered up in a white cast, which drew the attention of the two people opposite him. Darren and Nesta both breathed a sigh of relief, whilst Nick appeared to be bitterly disappointed.

"I thought you were Anwen," said Nick.

"We thought *you* were Anwen," said Nesta. "You scared the life out of us."

Darren paced around the room with his arms folded. "I wasn't even a tiny bit scared," he said.

Nesta took another look at the cast. "You poor thing," she said. "That must have been a nasty fall."

A weary Nick nodded. "I suppose some might say it was self-inflicted."

"I blame those two idiots in the audience," Nesta snapped. "They were so rude."

Nick nodded again. "You get used to people like that. We're not in Tennessee now. Not everyone who comes is going to love the show."

"Still, I think people need to give every live performer some respect. It's not easy getting up on that stage and performing. I know I'd have a hard time controlling the nerves."

The musician smiled. "If only all audience members were like you."

Darren chuckled at the mere idea of a venue full of retired teachers. "Good luck trying to do some crowd surfing in *that* gig!" He saw that Nesta was not nearly as amused and stopped grinning.

"I don't think I'll be doing any crowd surfing anytime soon," said Nick, gazing down at his foot.

"How serious are we talking?" asked Nesta.

"They said I've fractured my lateral malleolus," said Nick.

"Sounds nasty," said Darren with a wince.

Nick nodded. "I've no idea what any of that really means but it feels as horrible as it sounds. I've got to keep this thing on for at least six weeks." He lifted up his cast.

"But your big concert..." Nesta couldn't help but be worried about the man's showcase event at the local theatre. Surely, a country singer couldn't perform on crutches, she thought.

"The timing couldn't have been worse," said Nick with a grave face. "I've had some blows in my career — and I mean a few — but this one's probably up there."

Nesta watched the disappointed man hang his head and suddenly felt sorry for him. She had even forgotten her surroundings, as she tried to think of something positive. "How are you supposed to go up and down stairs with those?" She stared at the crutches. "Surely you need help."

"I've been bed-bound all afternoon," said Nick with a shrug. "Luckily, the bathroom's on the same floor as my room. Richard Neville and his son helped me up the stairs earlier. They said to call out if I need anything. I haven't seen anyone since." He let out an embarrassed cough. "That's actually why I hoped you were Anwen. I was hoping for a sandwich or something."

"You poor thing," said Nesta. "How could they leave an immobile guest to fend for themselves like that?"

NIck appeared to be enjoying the sympathy and continued to pull his miserable expression.

Darren let out a yawn. It had been a long day. "Yeah, that's a real shame, that." He turned to Nesta. "Right, shall we make a move and find some dinner? I'm starving!"

Nesta threw him a furious scowl, as Nick began scanning the room. "Wait," he said. "What are you two doing in here, anyway?"

The other two glanced at each other and were struck by a sudden sense of urgency.

"Never mind about that," said Nesta, rushing over to him. "Let's get you something to eat."

NICK SAT BACK against his pillow and munched on his dry ham sandwich. Nesta sat by his bedside, having struggled to find the ingredients in the downstairs kitchen. Even the age of the bread had been questionable, but Nick didn't seem to mind.

Darren was sitting on the other side of the bed in a sulk and couldn't work out why nobody had made *him* a sandwich. If a broken foot was all it took, he was quite willing to jump out the window for something to eat.

Nick continued to make chirpy noises, as he ate and ignored the pile of crumbs building up on his chest. As he finished the last morsel, the man had a face like a helpless toddler. "Any chance of desert?" he asked. "Anwen normally does something sweet with a cup of tea."

Nesta was about to tell the musician not to push his luck,

when she restrained her outburst and forced out a warm smile. "Oh, I'm sorry, Nick. The fridge was bare."

"Ah," said Nick with a nod. "Fair enough." She turned to the moody teenager. "Although, I'm sure Darren wouldn't mind making us all a cup of tea?"

"You — what?" Darren stared at her as though she had gone mad.

"Milk and one sugar, please. There's a good lad."

"Oh," said Nick, quickly perking up. "I'll have the same. But with five extra sugars."

"Five?!" Darren cried.

Nesta placed a hand on the man's shoulder. "He's right, you know. That's a terrible insulin spike for this time of day. It's not good for you."

"Oh, yeah." Darren folded up his arms. "That's exactly what I was worried about — the guy's health!"

"Actually," said Nick, leaning over and whispering. "Better make it two sugars. And see if you can find that biscuit tin she keeps."

"I'll find you that biscuit tin," Darren muttered, heading out of the room. "Hopefully it's full so I can hit someone over the head with it."

They watched him march out and slam the door.

"Never mind him," said Nesta. "You know what teenagers are like. They're up and down like a fiddler's elbow."

Nick chuckled. "It's been a long time since I was one of those."

"Do you have children?" Nesta asked.

The man shook his head. "Never even got married. It's not easy when you've been a working musician all your life. I've never settled anywhere, always moving around, doing any gig I can get — at least in the early years. There's no room for a love life." He paused. "Although, I did have a girlfriend once. After not seeing her for almost four months — long distance relationship and all that — I came back home to find out that she'd taken off without me even realising it. Turns out she'd left me three months before I found out."

"Wow," said Nesta, who didn't know what to say.

"Yeah," said Nick. "Imagine trying to marry *that* guy." He looked towards the window. "Sometimes I think to myself — there's a woman out there — my future wife. Somewhere, out in that big world is a woman who's busy living her life — not realising that she's going to spend the rest of it with me! That poor woman!" He let out a wild laugh. "Isn't that tragic?"

"Now, now." Nesta scratched her head. "You mustn't think like that."

Nick nodded. "You're right. I need to be more positive."

"It's just reality. Not everyone ends up with a soul mate. We should never presume that we're all going to get married. Some people never find love."

Nick was stunned by her frankness. "Oh. Thanks. That's reassuring to know." The man sighed and stared up at the ceiling. "I suppose I'll always have the love of the music."

Nesta thought about the musician's performance the other night and hoped that he and the music had signed a prenuptial agreement. "You seemed to be very close to Dale. I heard he was something of a mentor."

"He was more than a mentor," said Nick. "I'd say he was a good friend. Lord knows they're hard to come by in showbusiness. Everyone is usually out for themselves. But Dale was good to me. He was the real deal. The guy had been around enough to know who was genuine, and he could see right through people. Dale was my hero in many ways. I would have been more than happy to have had a career like his."

"It wasn't all plain sailing," said Nesta. "At least, I get the impression he wasn't at the peak of his success when he died."

Nick scoffed. "Success... now *there's* a word. Dale had integrity right to the end. He was a true artist — a proper musician. Success for him was playing a good gig. It wasn't about record sales or money deals. That's why I looked up to him."

Nesta thought about the man from the record label who was going to the big concert. "So, your injury isn't much of a setback at all?"

"Well," said Nick with a blush. "There's no harm in selling a few records if the opportunity's going. A guy's got to eat."

"Quite," said Nesta with a cynical nod. "I spoke with Dale's band members. They didn't seem to be mourning the loss of their leader very much. And that Noel is an ambitious character."

Nick's expression soured. "Don't talk to me about that sellout and his band of merry traitors. We were talking about integrity. Noel wouldn't know what that was if it smashed him in the face with his own guitar."

"You don't get on, then, I take it."

"On? They stabbed my friend in the back."

"In what way?" asked Nesta. She was aware that Dale was struck in the back of the head with a blunt object and assumed that the stabbing was a figure of speech (but she could never be sure).

"Dale wasn't stupid," said Nick. "He knew there was a mutiny going on. Noel and his minions had been in talks about forming a new band way before Dale was out of the picture. Course, they didn't have the guts to tell it to his face."

"How wicked of them," said Nesta.

"Like I said — showbiz is full of snakes. There aren't many of my kind still around."

"And what kind is that?"

Nick turned to her as though she hadn't been listening to a

word he had said. "A real country singer, obviously. I learnt from the best. And that best learnt from all the greats."

"That best being Dale Benham?"

"Of course!" Nick paused and realised that his voice had become very loud. "Sorry... as you can see — I can get very passionate when it comes to country music."

Nesta couldn't help but wonder about something she had discovered earlier that day and was trying to work out how to broach the subject without bursting the man's bubble. "Are you aware that Dale didn't write any of his own songs?"

The room went silent. Nick stared at her, and she tried to work out whether he was hearing this news for the first time or just shocked that she knew the truth. "Where did you hear that?" he asked, eventually.

"I assume it's common knowledge, isn't it?" Nesta cleared her throat. "I mean, don't get me wrong, I was personally quite shocked when I found out. I would have expected that someone as talented as Dale would write his own music. His songs had always come across as being very personal."

Nick did not respond and looked as though her words were stabbing him in the chest. Just as he was about to open his mouth to speak, they were interrupted by the sound of a falling mug.

"Damn it!" Darren cried, standing in the doorway with a tray of hot drinks. He looked down at the puddle of tea on the floor. "That one was yours, Nesta."

Knowing the extent of Darren's tea preparation skills, Nesta was secretly relieved. She only ever accepted a tea from him out of politeness and had become very proficient at hiding her disgust when taking that first sip.

"Never mind," she said. "At least Nick can still enjoy his." The poor man, she thought. Nobody deserved to suffer one of Darren's special brews.

Once he had handed out his delivery, Darren headed over to the guitar leaning against the set of drawers.

Nick watched the young man study his instrument. The teenager looked like an archaeologist who had just cracked open his first tomb. "She might need tuning. That fall off the stage didn't do my guitar any good, either."

Darren picked up the instrument and began plucking the strings. "Ooh, yeah. That sounds well out of tune."

"That's just the way you're playing it," said Nesta with a cheeky smirk.

The teenager pulled out his tongue. "I could play just fine if I knew the chords. I think I know one of them." He began curling his fingers across the fretboard and turned to the man lying in the bed. "How many more are there?"

"Thousands," said Nick before pausing to think about it. "In fact, I think the number is technically infinite."

"How many do you know?" asked Darren.

"A few." The musician took a gulp of his tea and almost gagged. "But you don't need all that many. In fact, the genre of country music is quite accessible to beginner guitarists. A lot of the songs are made up of a small number of basic major and minor chords. But knowing the chords is just the beginning." He sat up and signalled for him to pass him the guitar. "Here, I'll show you..." Nick formed a series of three chords with his left hand. "Good job I didn't break any of my hands, eh?" He chuckled to himself and began strumming. "Start with these three — A minor, C and G — and you've got yourself one of the most famous country songs of all time."

Nesta began bobbing her head in time with his strumming. "Oh! I recognise that!" She closed her eyes and began to sing: "Jolene... Jolene... Jolene, Joleeene!"

Darren scrunched up his face. "Who the hell is Joe Lean?"

The other two looked at each other and took pity on the young man.

"Here," said Nick, passing him back the guitar. "You have a go."

After a good twenty minutes of struggling to remember the positions of his new chords, Darren finally managed to produce a sound that didn't make his audience of two cringe. "Hey!" he cried. "I think I've got it!"

Nesta and Nick began singing along to his wonky guitar riff, until the excited teenager pumped his fist in the air.

"Joe Green... Joe Green... Joe Green, Joe Greeeeen!" He let out a proud smile. "I have no idea who that bloke is — but it sounds awesome!"

The other two tried not to let his gap in knowledge disturb them, and Darren continued jamming on the guitar.

"You know who that used to belong to?" Nick eventually asked. "And, before you say it, no, it wasn't Joe Green."

"I assume it's not Dale's," said Nesta. She studied the old guitar and could see that it had some serious mileage. "We saw his guitar in the other bedroom."

"It was once played by the legendary Bill Monroe," said Nick. He saw that the two faces looking back at him were completely blank. "Bill was known for being the father of bluegrass music."

"Was he really?" asked Nesta, who was genuinely fascinated. She had an uncle who was an enormous bluegrass fan and often could be seen strumming his banjo down at the local pub.

"The genre was named after Bill's band: The Blue Grass Boys." Nick pointed at the guitar. "That was made in the great state of Kentucky. Or, at least, that's what the man at the guitar shop told me, right?" He sniggered. "Still, I like to think that Bill used to bash on those strings. You want to borrow it?"

Darren looked up to check who he was referring to. "Who — me?"

"You seem to be getting very friendly with her. How about you hold on to it for the rest of your trip. Practise those chords."

"Uh, sure. Thanks." Darren was not used to such friendly gestures. The last item he had borrowed off someone was a murder mystery book from Nesta, and he gave the man an appreciative nod.

"I do hope you get back on your feet soon," said Nesta. "It's a shame we never got to see you perform at your best."

"Best?!" Nick laughed. "Please don't judge me on that performance at the pub. I was as drunk as a skunk. The word embarrassing doesn't even quite do it justice."

Nesta agreed: it was one of the worst performances she had ever witnessed. "Forgive me," she said, "but why drink so much before a gig? That can't be helping."

Nick hung his head and was already embarrassed about what he was about to admit. "I, uh... I've started getting... nervous."

"Nervous?"

"About going on stage." The musician avoided eye contact and began twiddling his thumbs. "It only started happening in the last couple of years. It's become like a condition. Out of nowhere, as soon as I'm about to go on stage, I'm struck by this crippling anxiety. It scared me at first. Normally, a little bit of nerves is a good thing. It shows you still care, and they keep you sharp. But this is something else completely. There was this one gig where my fingers couldn't even move. So I started having a drink or two to calm the nerves."

"What do you think is causing it?" asked Nesta.

The musician sighed. "I don't know. A loss in confidence, maybe? A fear of failure? Who knows. My career's not exactly gone from strength to strength over the last few years. I must have scared my subconscious." He stared at the white cast around his foot. "Maybe I should take a hint. It might be time to call it a day."

Nesta saw the gloominess in his face. It was hard for her to watch a man feel so broken, so sorry for himself. Even Darren was struggling to listen. This was not the Nick Franklin he had met on their first day at the lodge. He was beginning to prefer the proud, self-promoting Nick who had been quite happy to talk about his achievements at great length (even if most of it was highly exaggerated). This was a musician who had lost his fire, and it was quite painful to watch.

"Well," said Nesta, after their conversation had run dry. "I guess we should probably leave you to get some rest." She stood up and nodded at Darren.

They were just about to head back to their rooms, when Nesta remembered something. "Oh," she said, rushing back to his bedside. "Before we go, do you have any idea who this young lad might be?" She pulled out the photograph from Dale's room and showed it to him.

Nick leant forward and peered at the image of the young boy in the photograph. He smiled and nodded. "Yeah, I know who that is."

Nesta and Darren stared at him, as he took his time in revealing the identity.

"That's Dale's son."

CHAPTER 18

Nesta stared at her cooked breakfast, shaking her head. It had been her third fry-up of the trip, and she could feel her arteries about to burst. But it wasn't the sight of another plate of hearty ingredients that was disturbing her *that* morning.

"I still can't believe it," she said with a sip of strong tea.

Darren was munching away opposite her on his toast with chocolate spread. His father would have had a field day if he'd known what he was eating for breakfast, but now he was on holiday (and what happened in Barmouth, stayed in Barmouth). "It's not *that* surprising," he mumbled with a mouthful of toast. "Dale was old enough to be a grandfather. He probably has loads of kids."

"This is a bit different," said Nesta, who wanted to tell the young man to not talk with his mouthful. "Nick said that his son lives in the Barmouth area. I knew that half of Dale's ancestors hail from this neck of the woods, but I had no idea that he fathered a child here. And I say child — Nick seems to think that photo was taken decades ago. Which means that the boy is a grown man now." She shook her head again. Nick had gone on to tell them that Dale had shown him the photo when the two first met. The boy had been described as his firstborn and went by the name of "Bud" which was seemingly a nickname given to him by his estranged father.

"That festival director mentioned Dale had a relationship with a woman from Barmouth," Nesta added. "She could be the mother."

Darren was still enjoying his toast and didn't seem to be nearly as intrigued as Nesta. "Who cares? We're not here to cover Dale's family tree. Our viewers don't care about the murder victim's next of kin. Not unless they want to be put to sleep. They care about who killed the guy."

"Oh, for goodness sake..." Nesta began tutting. "Haven't you learnt anything yet?"

The teenager frowned. He was not in this partnership to receive lessons from a retired teacher and had no intention of "learning anything" — especially during the school holidays. "What do you mean?"

"I mean," Nesta snapped, "murders are often committed by those closest to the victim." She realised that her voice was now raised, and the elderly men on the table nearby turned to look at her. She smiled back and whispered her next words: "Every detective worth their salt starts with the family and friends."

Darren shuddered and glanced down at the knife and fork in her hand. If what she said was true, then he needed to keep a close eye on Nesta's eating utensils. "Okay, fine. So why would someone murder their own father?"

Now it was Darren's voice that was raised, and his loud question caused the two men to look away in fright.

"Money, usually." Nesta sliced into her bacon. "Inheritance is often a key motive, as cold as it sounds."

"But Dale was pretty broke, wasn't he?"

The teenager had raised a good point, Nesta thought.

Nobody with great wealth would have chosen to spend their nights under the roof of Anwen Neville. "His mother had recently passed away. I know she had quite a large estate over in Texas. It sounds like Dale had made his own way in life and was no stranger to sleeping rough and living a minimal existence. But things might have changed when he inherited his mother's wealth."

"Then why wasn't he living in a penthouse somewhere?" Darren asked. "That's what I'd be doing. Not busking around Barmouth."

Nesta shrugged. "Old habits die hard. People like what they're used to. And Dale was a working musician." She began tucking into her cold breakfast, when they were joined by their usual café attendant.

"Howdy, campers!" Sandy was dressed in a pink cowboy hat and struck a pose that Wonderwoman would be proud of. "Can I get ya'll some coffee refills?" She saw the blank expressions and reverted back to her native Welsh accent. "Tough crowd this morning. Can you tell that I'm not really a fan of country music?"

"I'll have a refill," said Nesta, lifting up her empty mug.

"I was joking," said Sandy. "We don't do free refills. Old Scrooge over there would have a heart attack." She pointed at her boss, Hywel, who was busy cooking over a hot stove. "I can get you another coffee, though."

"If you don't like country music," said Darren, "why bother with the hat?"

Sandy rolled her eyes. "Because if I don't do what my lord and master tells me, I don't get paid. We're the proud sponsors of *The Barmouth Country and Western Festival*, remember?"

Darren huffed. "I wouldn't let my boss tell me what to wear."

"Since when did you work a real job?" asked Nesta. "And I'm not counting my market stall."

"This woman was your boss?" asked Sandy with an excited smile.

"She's not my boss," Darren snapped. "Nobody is. I don't let anybody boss me around."

"That's why he's never the one paying the bill," Nesta whispered. "Young man doesn't know he was born."

Sandy let out a laugh, which only irritated Darren even more. "You seem like someone who likes to stick it to the man," she teased, gazing down at his heavy metal t-shirt. "Proper rebel, eh?"

"Oh, he likes to think so." Nesta could feel the teenager glaring at her. "But he still likes his bowl of *Rice Crispies* and comics before bed."

The two women giggled.

"Alright, alright." Darren frowned. "At least I'm not the one dressed like Dolly Parton."

"How do you know about Dolly?" asked Nesta.

"I looked her up last night on *Wikipedia*," Darren muttered. "Figured I might as well, seeing as I'm learning one of her songs. Looks like she did alright."

"Bless him," said Sandy, ruffling the young man's hair. "Isn't he sweet?"

Darren did his best to place his hair back the way he liked it.

"So what music do you like?" Nesta asked the young woman.

Sandy shrugged. "I like allsorts, me. But I was a bit of a punk in school."

"Punk?!" Darren did a double-take of the woman in the pink cowboy hat. "You like *punk*?"

"Don't sound so surprised," said Sandy. "You're not the only rebel in town. I liked a bit of heavy metal, too, actually." She pointed down at his t-shirt. "I was listening to *Iron Maiden* when you were still in nappies."

The embarrassed teenager shook his head and turned his focus back to the food on his plate.

"It feels very busy this morning," said Nesta, looking around the small café.

"Tell me about it," said Sandy. "My feet are killing me already, and the big man's in a bad mood. I keep telling that slave driver we need another pair of hands, but he's too tight-fisted." She looked over at a table in the corner of the room. "He's just stressed because we've got royalty here this morning."

Nesta turned to see the newly-titled Golden Wanderers gathered around the table. Noel and his band members were all silent whilst tucking into their breakfasts. "He's nervous about *that lot*?" she asked and checked her watch. "I'm surprised they're even out of bed at this time."

"You know this band?" Sandy asked.

Nesta lifted up her chin as though she was very well connected in the music industry. "Well, you know. I tend to rub shoulders with a few musicians these days."

Darren rolled his eyes. "What? Like ones who fall off the stage and break their feet?"

"I wouldn't call those four a fully-fledged band," said Nesta, ignoring the young man's effort to burst her bubble. "They're missing the one who made them known in the first place."

Sandy waited for her to elaborate. "Who's that?"

"Wow," said Nesta. "You *really* don't know your country music, do you?"

"Quite honestly?" Sandy turned to make sure her boss wasn't listening. "I couldn't give a damn. I only listen to the stuff because John Wayne over there insists we have it playing. It's like working in a shop during Christmas. After a while, you can't even hear the Christmas hits any more."

Nesta pointed towards the musicians in the corner. "They used to be Dale Benham's backing group."

"Ahhhhh…" Sandy groaned. "Rest in peace and all that. I've had enough of that guy too."

"Enough to murder him?" asked Darren.

"Darren!" Nesta cried. "How could you say such a thing?" She leant towards Sandy and lowered her voice. "But, in all seriousness, do you hate him enough to batter him on a bridge and leave him for dead?"

Sandy laughed. "You two really are a right funny pair! What are you? Private detectives?"

Her customers both looked at each other.

"It's a long story," said Darren.

"Well," said Sandy, who was having the most fun she'd had all morning, "I'd batter a few of his records first." She turned to glance behind the counter, where Hywel was giving her a dirty look. "And if there was anyone I *was* going to murder this month, it would be the gentleman over there."

Nesta nodded. It was fair enough, she thought. Hywel did not seem like a boss she would have liked, either. "Does your boss like Dale Benham?"

"Course he bloody does!" Sandy groaned. "Good job Dale's not here or Hywel would be all over him like a fangirl. We had him in a couple of times, actually." She now had both of their full attention.

"Alone?" asked Nesta.

Sandy shook her head. "Not always. The guy never actually had anything to eat. He only ever had a coffee, and I reckon that was only because it was on the house."

"Sounds about right," Darren muttered, fully aware of Dale's frugal spending habits.

"Who did he come in with?" asked Nesta.

The café worker tried to think. "There were a couple of people. This one time, he had coffee with Susan from the gallery round the corner. Talk about awkward. They had *definitely* slept together I reckon."

Nesta nodded. "Sounds about right. Anyone else?"

"Just some bloke I never met."

That could have been his manager, Nesta thought to herself. "Did you grow up in Barmouth, Sandy?"

"I've been here all my life. I should probably do something about that." Sandy sniggered. "Or I'll end up working for Hywel forever."

An excited Nesta reached into her handbag. "Then you might know who this is," she said and pulled out the photograph.

Sandy sighed. "Oh, I know everyone around here, for better or for worse. If there's gossip you need, I'm your woman."

"That's handy to know," said Nesta, showing her the photo from Dale's room. "Any ideas?"

The young woman stared at the image and smiled. "Any ideas? Yeah, course. I know that kid. He went to my school."

Even Darren was a little excited by this point. Maybe that raid of Dale's possessions *had* paid off after all, he thought.

"Well?" Nesta asked again.

Sandy held the photograph and continued to stare at the familiar boy. "Look how young he looks there. I feel old now." She handed it back to Nesta and prepared to rush off back to the counter. "That's Gethin Moore. A local farmer from across the bridge."

CHAPTER 19

Nesta and Darren looked out at the busy beach whilst licking their fresh ice creams. Hari sat in between them on the bench, waiting to catch some of the melted droplets on his hot tongue. Nesta wouldn't normally be eating ice cream in the first half of the day, but there was something about a cooked breakfast that always gave her a craving for something sweet (and, besides, she was on holiday).

"I just can't believe it," she said for the fourth time.

Darren nodded. "I know what you mean. I was expecting at least a flake for that price."

"Not the ice cream," Nesta snapped. "I'm talking about Gethin Moore."

"Oh," said Darren, still annoyed about his lack of chocolate. "Yeah, that was a weird one."

"Weird?! It doesn't make any sense!" She let Hari lick her sticky finger. "How can Gethin Moore be Dale Benham's son? He said his father was a farmer, and his mother, well... I suppose that could still be the gallery owner."

"Why are you so sure about the mother?" Darren asked. He

bit off the bottom of his cone and began sucking out the ice crime like a straw.

"I'm not sure about anything anymore."

They ate the rest of their ice creams in silence.

"Maybe Gethin wasn't talking about his biological father," said Darren, eventually. "Just because Dale was his real father, doesn't mean he called him that. I know people at school who live with step dads and mams. Sounds like Dale wasn't exactly around very much."

Nesta remained silent. She knew the teenager was right. It was easy to let a surprise revelation cloud her judgement and not everyone in the world grew up in the same situation as her. But Gethin Moore? *The son of Dale Watson? That* would take some getting used to.

"We might need to pay him another visit," she said.

Darren thought about having to make that long trek across the estuary again and groaned. "Seriously? Aren't we allowed to have just a little fun?"

"We already have," said Nesta. "We did the little train... we played golf..." She turned to see the young man's dissatisfied face. "What more do you want?"

"How about, today, we do something that I want to do for a change?"

Nesta lifted up her half-eaten cone. "What do you call this? We've just had ice cream."

"The ice cream was *your* idea!"

"Okay, fine." Nesta sighed. "So what do *you* want us to do that's so much fun?"

Darren had a twinkle in his eye, as he pictured their next move.

THE CLANKING SOUND beneath her feet caused Nesta to take a long, deep breath. As the caterpillar rollercoaster reached its summit, she braced herself for a sharp descent. The scream that came out of her mouth caused the teenager beside her to cringe, as he could have quite easily taken a nap on this "kiddie ride".

The multicoloured carriages flung around the winding track, and the passengers onboard were treated to an elevated view of the Barmouth seafront.

Darren felt a hand begin to squeeze his arm, and he pulled it away. "Aw! What are you doing?!"

Nesta was still tense and tried to control her breathing, as they reached another bend. She would have taken the Fairbourne Express over a fairground ride any day of the week. "I hope this is over soon."

The teenager let out a yawn. "Really? Don't tell me this ride is too much for you. Your driving's scarier than this." He felt another pinch and cried out again.

Once they had ground beneath their feet again, the next activity was a few laps on the dodgems. If Darren had thought Nesta's driving was reckless in her *own* vehicle, he soon discovered that Nesta in a bumper car was a whole different level of torture.

"Let me do the driving!" he wailed, grabbing hold of the steering wheel. "I knew we should have got separate cars..."

The next stop on Darren's "fun" tour was the amusement arcade, a place that Nesta had previously ventured on her trip to Talacre.

This time, instead of spending her money on penny pushers and slot machines, she found herself holding a plastic machine gun in front of a screen full of bloodthirsty zombies.

"Shoot!" Darren cried. "Shoot that one, over there!"

"I'm *trying* to shoot!" Nesta cried back (a sentence she never thought she'd utter). "There's too many of them!"

Despite the graphic violence, Nesta found herself opening fire like a Hollywood, eighties action star. It was amazing how a person could forgo their usual morals for blood and vengeance when there was a high score at stake.

"Yeah!" Darren clapped his hands. "You got him!"

Nesta let out an unexpected, maniacal laugh, as she finally shot down a giant monster, who, for reasons unbeknownst to her, wanted to eat her alive. After a few more kills, the numbers on the score counter caused both of them to leap into a victorious high-five.

"I told you this was fun," said Darren. The woman beside him was now trying to catch her breath.

"I would call it more of a cardiovascular exercise," said Nesta, leaning her weight against the side of the machine to recover her nerves. "I always thought video games were supposed to be a sedentary activity."

Hari was wagging his tail, as he could sense the excitement in the air.

"So what's next?"

Darren looked around the arcade like a giddy schoolboy. "Ready to fight it out to the death? There's a *Street Fighter* game over there!"

Nesta took another deep breath. "I think I've had my fill of blood and guts for one day." She caught sight of a penny pusher on the other side of the room. "I'll tell you what," she added, handing him some coins. "You go ahead without me. My treat. I need to catch up with an old friend."

The teenager gladly accepted the coins and headed off for more action.

Nesta and Hari made their way through a barrage of noise and lights, until they reached a window to a pile of two-pence pieces. This pile of pennies appeared to be hanging on by a thread, and Nesta was ready to be the lucky person to tip them over the edge. She rubbed her hands together and began entering a series of coins. After using up the last of her change, she let out a frustrated grunt. The coins were hanging tough, and Nesta was about to give the machine a little nudge, when she saw a familiar figure over by the slot machines.

"The house always wins, you know?"

Kris Neville paused his losing streak and looked up to see Nesta Griffiths standing beside him. He smirked and turned his attention back to the lemons and watermelons. "Tell me something I *don't* know."

"Very well," said Nesta sitting down at the slot machine beside him. "How about this — did you know that Gethin Moore is Dale Benham's son?"

Kris saw his credit turn to zero again and sighed. "Sure. But I wouldn't go telling Gethin that. He used to say the guy was dead to him." He paused to consider his choice of words and sniggered. "I guess he doesn't have to go saying that anymore. His dream's come true."

"I thought you didn't know Gethin all that well?" Nesta asked, having lost the patience of her first conversation with this young man.

"Nobody knows Gethin all that well," said Kris. "Not even Gethin."

"You seemed to make out that you weren't really friends."

Kris nodded. "How do you define *friend*? Someone who comes round once a week to play? Come on, adults don't really have *friends*. Just because I have beers with some guys down the local pub doesn't make them *friends*. Plus, you don't want to go around saying that you're Gethin Moores' friend — not when there's coppers knocking on your door asking questions."

Nesta was beginning to understand why Kris Neville didn't consider himself to have many friends. "What do you mean by that?"

The man began slipping in another load of coins into his machine and pressed the buttons like he could do it on auto-pilot. "Like I said before, it doesn't take a detective to know that Gethin Moore's dodgy. The guy's got a criminal record, and he's just bought a new *Jaguar Land Rover*. What does that tell you? You'd need a lot of sheep to buy one of those."

"Maybe he came into some inheritance," said Nesta.

Kris laughed. "Yeah, sure. That's a good one. He should tell the police that when they come knocking."

Nesta shook her head in frustration. "Alright, so between us, you obviously *do* know the man quite well."

"No more than all the other guys down at the pub," Kris muttered.

"Then how do you know about his biological father?"

The man didn't answer and continued to focus on the machine, until Nesta reached across and pressed one of his buttons.

"Hey!" he cried out.

The machine let out a loud, upbeat jingle before Kris' credit shot up.

"Sorry," said Nesta. "It's all about the timing with these things."

Kris groaned. "Alright, so Gethin did some work for me a while back. Again, doesn't make us best mates, though, does it?"

Nesta sensed a disdain in the man's voice. Something told her that there was some tension between the two men. "Work?"

"Gethin was struggling to find work because of his criminal record. His farm wasn't doing so well, and he needed some extra income coming in. So I offered him the chance to do some jobs for me. I was really busy at the time and needed the extra pair of hands. He was a good worker, to be fair. And you know how it is when you're working with someone everyday. You learn more about your work colleagues sometimes than you do about your girlfriend. He mentioned that this Dale fella had been trying to make contact again. They'd done a DNA test and everything to make sure. But Gethin still considered Owen to be his real father."

"Was Owen the owner of the farm he lives on now?" asked Nesta. "The man who died?"

Kris nodded. "Yeah, tragic, that. Gethin had taken Owen's death really hard. He was technically his step dad, but the guy had raised Gethin since he was born. No wonder the guy went off the rails and all that." He cursed at the sight of another loss on his machine.

"So, how do you think Gethin is making so much money? The man's playing golf in expensive looking clothes and all sorts."

The man beside her laughed. "Is he really? The flash git! What an idiot. You don't flaunt your cash around like that. Not when you're in the type business *he's* in."

Nesta stared at him. "So you *do* know what he's up to? Why he's so successful..."

"Successful?!" Kris slammed his fist down on one of the flashing buttons. "There's only one reason he's successful, and it's got nothing to do with *him*." He took a deep breath and tried to calm his nerves. All the dopamine from his lengthy session on the slot machines was starting to make him irritable and erratic. "Yeah, I know how he makes his money. I was there when he got the idea." He leaned out of his chair and made sure that no one was nearby. "We went for some beers once after a job. It had been a right nasty, grubby one, too, and we were knackered. There we were at the bar, and this flash bloke from out of town was in there buying everyone drinks. He had a brand new *BMW* parked outside and was trying to impress these girls that were in there. Eventually, me and Gethin decided to join this guy and ask him what his secret was — what he did for a living and all that. Our clothes were all stained from the job we'd just finished, and we must have looked like a right pair of chancers. Turns out this guy was looking to franchise this business of his."

"Why does something tell me that this business wasn't exactly legal?" asked Nesta with a disapproving frown.

Kris laughed. "*Exactly* legal?! It wasn't legal in the slightest!" He suddenly realised how loud his voice had become and cupped his mouth. "Anyway, long story short, Gethin and I decided to jump on the guy's opportunity. We went into business together."

Nesta nodded. Suddenly, that animosity in Kris' tone was starting to make sense. If there was one thing she knew about this so-called business venture, it was that Gethin and Kris were no longer partners — and Kris wasn't the one driving the *Jaguar Land Rover*.

"I've told you far too much already," Kris said, looking a little nervous and shaky. He grabbed his jacket and prepared to make a quick exit. The time had run away from him (as it always did in that amusement arcade). "You know, love, you'd make a good copper. Has anyone ever told you that?"

Nesta smiled. "They may have done. But I've also been called nosey." She was a little disappointed not to hear the end of Kris' story, but she had a feeling he would not be the one to finish it. The man had left so quickly that he had forgotten about his remaining credit.

Nesta slipped into Kris' warm chair and Hari jumped up on her lap. All of a sudden, she was feeling rather lucky.

CHAPTER 20

"What could it be?" Darren asked, his mind bustling with ideas.

"It doesn't really matter what it is," said Nesta. "The point is — it's illegal. And that means he'll be dealing with all kinds of unsavoury characters."

They were both making their way back into town across the central railway crossing. Darren had used up the last of his coins on the grabber machines. His excuse had been to win a stuffed toy for Hari, but Nesta knew full well that the teenager just wanted to try and outsmart a clawing device that was rigged to beat him. The prizes had been there for the taking, and it all looked so easy on first glance. Darren had been adamant that he'd secured himself a stuffed warthog, only to watch it slip away in an instant. He would get it next time, he had assured himself.

"Aren't you just a little bit curious?" he asked.

"About what?" Nesta asked back. "You think I want to know the sordid details of Gethin Moore's business? Like I said, it doesn't matter. The point is that there's a lot of criminal activity going on in that farm, and Dale Benham's body was found just down the road."

"Maybe it's the Cartel. Or the Mafia?"

"I don't care if it's Al Capone," Nesta snapped. "In fact, I don't really want to know."

Darren smiled. "The viewers will."

"I bet they do." Nesta huffed. "They're like hungry vultures. But we didn't come to Barmouth to expose a criminal organisation. We came here to get to the bottom of what happened to Dale Benham, and I'm not leaving until we find out."

"You're the one normally saying we should explore every avenue. Earlier you were going on about Dale's extended family. You really want to turn a blind eye at a potential link to the criminal underworld?" Darren shook his head with frustration, as they began strolling down the high street.

Nesta went quiet for a moment. She knew he was right but normally tried to avoid telling him that if at all possible. She also had no desire to delve into the world of organised crime. Drugs or gangsters really weren't her thing, but perhaps, this time, she didn't have a choice.

"Alright," she said. "Fine. If you really think it's that important. But how on earth are we going find out what Gethin is really up to without rummaging around his farm? He knows who we are now and doesn't trust me in the slightest."

Darren's face lit up with excitement, as a lightbulb went off in his head. The bulb didn't come on very often, he would admit, but now he had come up with the perfect plan. "I've got a few ideas," he said.

Nesta looked back at him in horror. A Darren idea was never good, and she prepared to have her suspicions confirmed. "Go on..." Just as she was about to be enlightened by Darren's cunning plan, they came across an altercation going on over in the outside seating area of a busy pub.

Darren pointed towards the two men embroiled in a loud shouting match. "Isn't that —"

"Yes," said Nesta. "Yes, it is."

The group of musicians now known as The Golden Wanderers had been enjoying an afternoon pint with their manager. Now, their drummer, Stew, was nose-to-nose with a furious Robin, whilst other members of the band were trying to pull them apart.

"And there's our fellow internet sensation," Nesta added. She was referring to Kenny Leith, the man who was filming the entire argument on his mobile phone. The country-themed online influencer was in his element and didn't seem to be concerned about the two men's welfare.

Darren looked over at the man with his cowboy hat and extra-large t-shirt, lurking near the band like a persistent fly. "That's the guy with that channel you told me about? Doesn't seem to have much integrity."

"Or manners," Nesta muttered.

They both witnessed Eric, the double bassist, trying to push Kenny away and cover up his lens. Despite Kenny's intruding nature, Nesta revelled at the thought of rooting through the man's videos. He might come in useful yet, she thought.

"What could they be fighting about?" asked Darren.

Nesta let out an excited grin. "Let's get a little closer and find out."

They both scurried across the road like curious little mice, and when they reached the pub's outside barrier, the crowd of fellow spectators all let out a gasp.

Nesta and Darren froze, as Robin Lock went flying backwards into a row of chairs after being struck by a vicious blow to the jaw. A furious Stew towered over him with a sore knuckle and began hurling abuse at the man before storming off.

The rest of the band members rushed to Robin's aid and dragged him up from the floor.

"That's it!" Robin cried out. "I've had it! That man is out!! You hear me? Out!!"

Having enjoyed all of the commotion, an excited Darren turned to see that Nesta was already following the drummer up the street. He hurried after her with Hari by his side.

Further down the street, Stew marched along the pavement, his fists still clenched, until he made a sharp turn towards the entrance of a small gallery.

Nesta, who wasn't far behind, paused to wait for Darren and gazed up at the gallery's sign: *Peggy Sue's*.

"I wasn't expecting that," said Darren, as he tried to catch his breath. "I wonder what it was all about?" He saw that Nesta was still staring at the gallery. "Is that where he went? What, now he fancies looking at some paintings?"

"Noel talked about the drummer having a similar altercation with Dale, remember? Sounds like this Stew character has some serious temper issues. This gallery must belong to the woman Stew was having an affair with."

Darren scratched his head. "Wasn't this same person in a relationship with Dale?" He shook his head. These relationships were getting far too complicated for his tired brain to keep up with.

Nesta nodded. "She was supposedly the love of Dale's life. And, I would presume, the mother of Gethin Moore."

"Flippin' heck," said Darren. "Now my head's *really* spinning."

"That's probably all those rides we've been on," said Nesta. "I told you it wasn't a good idea."

The teenager ignored her comment and tried to remain focused. "So, how do you know this gallery belongs to this same woman, anyway?"

Nesta smiled and pointed at the sign. "The woman's name was Susan, and she owned a gallery. Luckily, Barmouth is a small town."

Darren stared at the name *Peggy Sue's* and nodded. "Now what? You seemed pretty keen on catching up with Stew considering he'd just knocked someone's block off."

"I wanted a quick word," said Nesta.

"Sure you did!" Darren laughed. "Well, I would give the guy a minute to cool down. He doesn't really seem in the mood for a chat." He turned to see that Nesta had already disappeared inside the gallery. Fortunately for him and Hari, there was a sign on the window that said *Dogs Welcome*.

The inside of *Peggy Sue's* was as spacious as a person would imagine for an art gallery. Its walls were as white as a blank canvas, and the floor had been polished so much that it resembled an ice rink. Nesta could understand why the owner had chosen such a minimalist design. With nothing around to distract the eye, a person could focus their eyes on what was important: the artwork hanging on the walls.

Darren was not nearly as impressed when he entered the large room and had no interest in browsing the range of paintings and photographs. "We're not going to be here long, are we?"

Nesta refused to answer his abrupt question and continued to admire a landscape formed out of acrylic paint. She immediately recognised the view, as she had witnessed the real thing earlier that day.

"That's Barmouth Bridge," said Darren, appearing over her shoulder. "Doesn't look very realistic, though."

Nesta sighed, her moment of being lost in the sea of colours broken. "It's not about being realistic. It's about capturing the moment."

Darren stared at the painting again and raised a cynical eyebrow. "Now you sound like my art teacher."

The former English teacher knew exactly the person he was referring to and did not appreciate being compared to *that* man. "Sounds like he hasn't exactly inspired you to look beyond what's in front of you."

The teenager shrugged. "He took us to some gallery in Liverpool once on a school trip."

"The *Tate*?"

"Yeah, that's what I thought of him too."

"I *mean*," Nesta said, "did you get to see the *Tate Modern*?"

"Not really," said Darren. "I snuck off to look round *John Lewis*. I needed to find some new jeans."

Nesta decided to not let the conversation go on any further and went back to admiring the painting. Darren sighed and wandered over to a giant photograph on the other side of the room. It captured the face of an elderly man in a tight close-up. As much as it had grabbed his attention, Darren could not fathom what was so hard about taking a photograph and placing it on the wall. After all, he was quite capable of doing that himself with his trusty mobile phone, but none of his recent images had been mounted for the world to see. Perhaps, he thought, it was worth getting one of his own photos framed and put on sale with a hefty price tag. He was quite certain that Nesta would be happy to volunteer her face.

"I see you've fallen in love with this man as much as I did," said a voice from over his shoulder.

Darren turned around to see a woman in a colourful headband hovering behind him. Susan Tapscott was about the same age as his mother and had a natural beauty that felt timeless.

"Love?" Darren asked with an embarrassed scoff. "I was just thinking he was a creepy old man."

Susan gazed at the photograph with a proud smile. She didn't seem to let the young man's scepticism bother her (the woman had been an artist for far too long to let something as trivial as *criticism* bother her). "I remember the day I took that photo like it was yesterday. It was down by the harbour. There was something about this gentleman I just had to capture: the rawness, the soul, the life…"

"The nose hair?" asked Darren.

The artist burst out laughing. "Yes, especially the nose hair. This is a warts-and-all portrait."

Darren turned around to get another full view of the gallery. "Did you make *everything* in this room?"

Susan nodded. "Almost everything. I've got a couple of pieces from local artists as well."

"And people actually pay you money for this stuff?"

"Darren!" Nesta joined them both by the photograph, frowning at her narrow-minded young companion.

"It's alright," said Susan. "I'm not offended. He's a very inquisitive young man."

"That's one word for it," Nesta muttered.

Susan stepped back to admire her own work. "And the answer is — yes. I do make a living from my craft. It's something I'm not ashamed to talk about. I would do it all for free, of course, but being able to make a living from your passion is a thrill like no other."

Darren was still baffled. "Don't get me wrong, like. You're a good painter. It's just…"

"Everything is so expensive?" Susan asked before letting out another laugh. "I'll take *good painter* as a compliment." She saw the young man starting to turn red.

"No, what I mean is — your painting's awesome —"

"Now he's trying to dig himself out of a hole," said Nesta. "You wouldn't think that he's an artist himself."

Susan turned to the teenager with a curious face. "You are?"

"I am?" asked Darren.

Nesta nodded. "He produces online videos. Well, we both do, actually."

"Ah, so you're a cinematographer?" asked Susan. "Interesting..."

Darren rather liked the idea of being called an artist and tried to save face by pretending to study the photograph again with more depth. "Uh, sure, yeah. I guess I am."

"Looks like we've got a lot in common," said Susan. "Our canvases might be different, but we're still trying to capture life and all its beauty."

Not so much the "beauty", Nesta thought. A dead corpse and a killer at large was hardly the brighter side of life. "I really love your painting of Barmouth Bridge," she said, pointing to the other side of the gallery. "It has a certain eerie quality with all the mist."

"Thank you," said Susan. "That's actually my most recent painting."

"Is that right?" Nesta asked. "What a funny coincidence."

The artist looked confused. "How do you mean?"

"Well, considering all the press attention that bridge has been getting recently."

Susan suddenly realised what she was referring to and nodded. "Ah, yes. Perhaps it was all subconscious — or maybe even a premonition? Who knows... the creative mind works in mysterious ways."

"It certainly does," said Nesta. "I believe you knew the man well."

The gallery owner was caught off guard for a moment. "Who, Dale? Uh, yes. I knew Dale. How did you know that?"

Nesta smiled. "It turns out we have a lot of people in common. Like your son, for instance."

Now Susan was even more surprised. "You know Gethin?"

The mere mention of the farmer's name gave Nesta a tingle

of excitement. Her suspicions were confirmed. "He's doing well for himself these days."

"Yes," said Susan, who had a sudden urge to leave the conversation and walk away. "He's doing okay."

"It can't be easy running that farm all on his own," Nesta continued.

"No, I suppose not. He takes after his father. The man was a good farmer."

"Owen?"

The artist peered back into this stranger's eyes. "I'm sorry, should I know who you are? I don't believe we've ever met."

Nesta paused to contemplate her next move. In the end, she had come to realise that it was usually easier to just be honest. "I'll be frank with you," she said. "Darren and I are not just in Barmouth for a holiday."

Susan folded up her arms. "I sort of gathered that." She turned to face Darren. "Teenagers don't usually go on holiday with their grandmothers. At least my one never would have."

Darren frowned and was about to protest when Nesta cut him off.

"We're investigating the murder of your former boyfriend, Dale Benham."

The artist scoffed. "There are two things wrong with that sentence. Firstly, you two don't look like police officers to me, and, secondly, Dale was certainly not my *boyfriend*."

For a moment, Nesta caught the spitting resemblance of her son. "I was under the impression that you've known each other a long time."

"I've known a lot of people in Barmouth for a long time," Susan snapped. "Doesn't mean I've dated them all." Her mood had become irritable, having hoped that the two people wandering around her art gallery would bring her a sale (not a conversation about her personal life).

"But Dale was not from Barmouth," Nesta corrected her.

"He would disagree," said Susan. "You know what Americans can be like — they find some ancestry in another country and they call it the homeland."

"His mother was born and bred here."

Susan rolled her eyes as though she had heard it all a thousand times. "Oh, yes. How could we forget about Lady Lydia? She also has a sibling and a whole lot of Barmouth relatives. I bet you didn't know that."

"Did you know that Lydia has passed away?"

Nesta's question left the woman stunned. She didn't even need a response. "She died?" Susan asked.

"Something tells me that you didn't know that," said Nesta. "I'm surprised that Dale didn't tell you."

The mention of Dale's name caused Susan's face to sour again. "Like I said, we weren't that close. At least, not anymore."

"But you *were* at one time?"

The artist checked her watch and searched for an excuse to leave. "Listen, I was young and naive when Dale Benham first came into my life. I didn't even know what love was back then. It was just a crush. But I soon got over that. It's a shame Dale didn't."

Nesta could sense that the woman's feelings towards the country singer were not what she had expected. There was a hatred there, and she had no intention of hiding it. "Did Dale love you?"

Susan gave her a serious stare. "There's a difference between love and obsession. That man just couldn't take no for an answer. Not even when I got married. Every time my life would start to settle down, he would just show up at my door as if I'd been waiting for him all along." She sniggered. "It was pathetic, really. But he never could take a hint. Eventually he tried suggesting Gethin was his son — as if that would ever bring us together. But even Owen didn't need a DNA test to tell who Gethin's real father was. Deep down, both of us always knew."

"Did all this affect your marriage?" asked Nesta.

"I didn't need Dale Benham to ruin *that* trainwreck," Susan snapped. "Not when I married a complete control freak. That farm of his was like living in a prison. The best thing I ever did was leave that place. As you can tell, I really know how to pick them."

Nesta could not disagree with her there. So far, the woman's track record had not been great. "And where does the drummer fit into all this?"

There was a long silence.

"I beg your pardon?"

"Stew is upstairs now, isn't he? I saw him walk in just after he punched his manager in the face." Nesta pointed to the ceiling. "Like you said — you really know how to pick them."

Susan shook her head in disbelief. "You have no idea what you're talking about. Stew is completely different to that psychopath."

The woman's choice of clinical definition surprised Nesta. "You think Dale was a psychopath?"

The artist laughed. "Let me guess — you know him as the warm, cuddly Texan? Like I said, you have no idea what you're talking about. Stew has been the only source of hope I've ever had in my life. He's a decent human being, someone who was always the voice of reason in that group." She turned her focus to a painting full of splattered reds and oranges. It was very abstract but clearly contained a lot of passion and anger. "He has a temper, sure. But he's a man of principle and dignity. Unlike most musicians. He's been a good friend."

Nesta dwelled on the word "friend". Even if Susan and Stew's relationship had indeed been plutonic, she suspected that Dale had not approved.

"Now," said Susan, turning back around to face her two visitors. "If you don't mind, I'd like you both to leave my gallery."

Nesta and Darren both looked at each other.

"Don't need to tell me twice," said the teenager, who had experienced more than his fair share of artistic culture for one day. He marched straight out of the room with Hari by his side.

Nesta took one last look at the fiery painting with its splattering of red paint and shuddered.

CHAPTER 21

"It's like something out of *Close Encounters*," said Nesta with a gasp. She watched the mysterious flying object whizz upwards in a perfectly straight line and hover up above as if it was about to beam her up.

"Have you really never seen one of these before?" Darren asked, clutching his controller.

Nesta stared up into the sky. "Not in real life. I've seen them on *The One Show*. But they look so much bigger in the flesh — and they're a lot nosier."

Darren's drone was now hovering above the halfway mark of Barmouth Bridge and possessed the best view in the entire estuary. At four hundred feet above bridge level, even the Cadair Idris mountain would struggle to compete with such a perfect aerial view of its surroundings. Luckily for the drone's pilot (a term coined by the operator himself), he could take in this view with the help of his trusty mobile phone app.

"You see," he said, as Nesta peered over his shoulder. "We can pinpoint an exact location on our map, and the drone will head there." He pointed at his small screen.

"How clever," said Nesta, who was slowly being won over. She had been initially reluctant to be involved in the operation of a device that was known to hover over people's garden fences and spy on unsuspecting members of the public, but now she was dying to grab the controls herself. "Right," she said, lifting up Dale's map. She placed her index finger on the mark he had made in the vast area of land on the other side of the bridge. "Do you think it can handle these coordinates?"

Darren turned to her and smiled. "This baby? Course she can handle it."

With a few taps of his fingers, Darren sent the drone flying off on its new mission.

Nesta watched the small screen with great fascination and saw the same landscape and terrain that she had recently crossed on foot, only now it was from a birds-eye-view. The large body of water down below had changed into grassy fields, and Nesta felt like she was hovering herself.

They would soon find out what treasures were located on Dale's map. If the X really did mark the spot, the drone would have no trouble revealing the outcome.

"What if he's buried something?" Darren asked, as they both waited in anticipation. "We're not going to see a thing."

"Why are you so obsessed with people burying things?" Nesta asked.

Darren was reminded of the dreaded hole in the Nevilles' back garden and shuddered.

The drone went soaring across a layer of trees and stopped abruptly above a stone structure down below.

"Here we go," said Darren. "She's reached the end destination."

Nesta was struck by the teenager's constant use of the word "she" when describing his precious toy and began to worry about how much time he was spending alone. She hoped that someday he would find himself a nice real female friend, one who wasn't made out of nuts and bolts (but that was a discussion for another time).

They both peered at the screen.

"It's a house," said Darren, lowering the drone to get a closer look. "Why would Dale be so interested in a house?"

"Maybe it's what's inside the house," said Nesta. "Can we go inside?"

Darren turned to look at her in disbelief. "I'll just get the drone to ring the doorbell as well, shall I?"

Nesta struck him with her folded map. "I thought this thing was supposed to be clever. Even I can just walk inside a house."

"But you can't fly around like Mary Poppins, can you?" Darren secretly suspected that the woman probably *could* if she had access to an umbrella. "This is supposed to be a stealth mission — a reconnaissance exercise — not a social visit."

Nesta sighed. "It's a complete waste of time if you ask me. What good is it if we can't have a look around?"

Darren shook his head and took to the controls. "Hang on." He manoeuvred his fingers and caused the flying object to lower itself, slowly, until it was the same height as the upstairs window. "I better not get arrested for being a peeping Tom."

The small cottage appeared to be very isolated and in dire need of a new roof. Its condition was so bad, Nesta was beginning to wonder if anyone even lived there at all. Even the front door was hanging on by a thread, and the front garden had been taken over by an invasion of weeds and long grass.

"I don't think anyone's home," Darren muttered.

"Wait," said Nesta, squinting at the small screen. "What's that above the front door?"

Her pilot steered the drone so that she could get a better look at the faded house name: *Blas Yr Halen*.

"The taste of salt..." Nesta deliberated over the Welsh name for a moment and pulled a pen out from her handbag. She scribbled down the name on the edge of her map. "You think you can Goggle that address?"

Darren didn't bother to correct her on the search engine name (he was used to it by now). "Sure, we can check it out."

Nesta nodded. "Time to bring her home," said Nesta with a nod. She had begun to liken the drone to a loyal falcon and prepared to welcome her back from the sky.

As Darren prepared to summon his pride and joy back again, he became tempted by a better idea. "How about we check what our farmer friend is up to?" He let out a mischievous wink and waited for Nesta's reaction.

"The last time we were over at Morwyn Farm, you couldn't wait to get out of there."

It was true — Darren had never liked farms, which was surprising given that he had grown up in a very rural area. His experience with the young farmers at school had mostly been confrontational, and they never seemed to like him very much either. Not being a farmer in the first place had made Darren different (and *different* was never a good thing for a person in the depths of adolescence). "Yeah," he said, waving his remote control. "But this time I'll be at a safe distance."

The drone hovered its way back in the direction of the estuary and made a detour to a certain farmhouse with its cluster of outbuildings.

"Look," said Darren, as they approached the outskirts of the property. "Someone's leaving."

They both witnessed a man walking to his car at the end of the drive. He was the biggest person that either of them had ever seen, a man with enormous muscles that made him resemble a transformer.

"Goodness," said Nesta. "What a big neck he has."

Darren nodded. "All the better to maul someone with," he muttered.

"Why would Gethin be associated with a brute like that?"

"Looks like he needs a lot of muscle on hand..."

The drone hovered over the farm yard for a while and waited for the large man to leave. Darren lowered the flying object until it was only a couple of metres from the ground. "I can't see anyone."

"That shed door's open," said Nesta. "See if you can get closer."

Darren licked his top lip whilst he tried to concentrate. He moved their camera lens closer to the open doorway and steadied the drone so that it could creep its way inside. The teenager's fingers were quivering by this point, and he felt beads of sweat begin to trickle down his forehead. "Steady..." He crossed through into what could only be described as a makeshift laboratory. Boxes were stacked high and, even in the dim light, it was clear that health and safety was not a priority in *this* facility, where test tubes and chemistry beakers were scattered across a series of tables. The descriptions on the various tubs of powders and ingredients were all in a foreign language, and the equipment reminded the teenager of his school science labs.

"I think this might be a bad idea," said Nesta in shock.

Darren nodded and steered the drone back in the direction of the doorway. Just as they saw the flash of daylight, a mysterious figure was now leaning over their shoulders back on the bridge.

"What we got here, then," said the deep voice.

The unexpected third presence caused Darren to drop his remote control, and, less than a mile or so away, the drone went crashing to the floor with a *thud*.

"Sorry," said Rhys. "I didn't mean to frighten you."

Nesta and Darren stared back at the sheepish-looking fisherman with his German Shepherd. They found it hard not to be cross with him, and, when they realised the screen had now gone black, both of them let out a gasp.

"Oh, no!" Nesta cried. "What happened?!"

"What do you think happened?" Darren asked, bashing the controls. "We've crashed it!"

Nesta let out a disgruntled huff. "I wouldn't say that I had any hand in that." She turned to the confused fisherman. "If it was *anyone's* fault..."

Rhys removed his woolly hat and scratched his head. "Who — me?"

"It doesn't matter now," Darren snapped. "We've lost her!"

The awkward fisherman decided it was best to keep his distance and returned to his usual post further down the bridge.

Nesta glanced over towards the south side of the estuary. "We haven't lost her *necessarily*."

THE FARMYARD WAS STILL empty when Darren and Nesta approached. Their view of the outbuildings were very different now that they were no longer viewing them through a wide angle lens.

Darren had preferred keeping his distance (about half a mile or so to be precise), but desperate times called for desperate measures, and he was not prepared to lose his precious drone that easily.

"It was that one over there," Nesta whispered.

They scurried across the yard and found the shed door still ajar. Nesta felt a surge of adrenaline (and, if she was being honest, rather enjoyed it). Darren, on the other hand, had no desire to waste any time and soon located his fallen baby.

The drone was lying in the corner of the room like a wounded bird, and the two trespassers were struck by a strong smell of chemicals. Whatever the farmer was cooking up in that room, it certainly was not for the faint-hearted.

Once Darren had grabbed his drone, he found Nesta snooping around the tables.

"We've not got time for that," he whispered.

"What do you think he's making?" Nesta asked, picking up a mysterious tub of powder.

"I couldn't give a monkey's at this point," said Darren. "He could be making magic potions for all I care. Come on, let's get out of here."

As Nesta and Darren re-emerged into the fresh air, they were faced with a person dressed in a boiler suit and dust mask. The mysterious figure caused them both to freeze, and Hari growled before letting out a bark. A pair of furious eyes glanced down at the drone in Darren's arms.

The man looked as though he was about to enter a radioactive facility and lowered his mask to reveal the face of Gethin Moore. "Welcome back," he said.

The intruders both looked at each other, helplessly. They had been caught red-handed, and there was no use denying otherwise.

"Gethin," said Nesta with a concerned expression. "What have you got yourself into?"

The farmer took a deep breath. "I would say that it's none of your business."

"You might as well tell us," said Darren, lifting up his drone. "We've caught everything on camera. What are we talking? Dope? The Cartel? Heroin?"

Gethin let out an enormous laugh. "You've been watching

too much telly. I'm sure I'd be a lot richer if any of those were true."

"Now, come on, Gethin." Nesta took a step forward and Hari let out another loud bark. "There's no use denying it. We know your little operation here can't be legal."

The farmer scoffed. "I ain't denying anything. And you're right — it's anything but legal. That's why there's so much money in it. But the way I look at it, it's nothing immoral. It's supply and demand. There's plenty of people who are ready to buy. I'm just giving the consumers what they want."

"So we're talking drugs?" Nesta asked.

"Drugs is a very broad term. But, sure, I guess they're technically drugs. I like to call them performance enhancers."

The pair in front of him were now even more confused. "Performance enhancers?"

"Steroids," said Gethin. "Nothing out of the ordinary in my industry. People use them on cattle all the time."

Darren scratched his head. "So... you're making steroids for sheep?"

Gethin laughed again and turned to Nesta. "Your lad's not the sharpest tool in the box, is he?"

"He's smart enough not to do what you're doing," Nesta snapped, defensively.

"Oh, yeah?" Gethin's jovial mood changed. "Do you know how much money I'm raking in doing this? It's a lot more than farming, I can tell you that."

"Let me guess," said Nesta. "Something to do with franchising from a bloke you met down the pub? Am I right?"

Gethin struggled not to look surprised. "Who you been talking to?"

"Your old friend — Kris Neville."

The farmer nodded. "Now it makes sense. The guy should

have taken the opportunity whilst he could. No wonder he's still bitter and skint."

Nesta thought about the man she had seen leaving his farm. He had been built like a bull on steroids, and she wondered if her suspicions were true. "These performance enhancers... are we talking people who spend a lot of time lifting weights?"

"Gym rats?" Gethin asked. "Yeah, I'd say that's probably my key demographic. Although, you get a lot of people who are willing to take the juice but aren't prepared to put the work in. Either way, I get paid anyway."

"Hang on," said Darren. "Steroids aren't illegal. I know a guy from Bala who's clearly on something."

"Anabolic steroids are a class C drug in this country," said Gethin. "They're legal to posses for personal or medical use. But they're illegal to produce and supply. Go figure! It's why this whole scheme is genius. Thanks to my mate down the pub, I can order all the ingredients from abroad and put them all together in my own back yard. It's like following a cake recipe. An idiot could do it!"

"I can see that," said Nesta.

Gethin frowned. "I don't even care if I get caught, either. You get about fourteen years. If I make enough money now and squirrel it all away, I'll be laughing by the time I get out."

Nesta gave him a pitiful stare. "Is this really what your life has come down to? You think this is the life Dale would have wanted for his own son?" She pulled out the photograph from her handbag and handed it to him.

Gethin's smug expression had vanished. He stared down at the small boy in the image and shook his head. "Where did you find this?"

"Your father's room," said Nesta. "From what I hear, he thought the world of his little boy."

There was a long silence, and Gethin tried his best to hide any hint of emotion. "He's no father of mine." He handed back the photo with a lump in his throat. "Dale Benham was a washed-up cowboy who died alone on that bridge. I never have to see his face again at my front door. Whoever finished him off did me a favour." He stared his two visitors down with a pair of teary eyes. "Now get off my land."

CHAPTER 22

Ryan Kirby, one the United Kingdom's biggest rising country music stars, stared at himself in the mirror and cringed. He had been *really* stitched up this time, he thought. This would be the last time he would accept a job outside of his manager, and he would be doing no more favours from now on.

His new album was almost finished, and he didn't have time to be slumming it in a tiny theatre on the Welsh coast. Ryan's cousin, Felix, had told him that this supposed "gig" would be the perfect opportunity to try out some of his new songs to a young and trendy crowd, and, instead, he had discovered a venue full of aging country and western fans — the type who liked to dress up in big hats and leather cowboy boots. He considered *his* style of country music to be worlds apart from the line-dancing, hoedown-inducing records of the past. Ryan considered himself a pioneer — an enabler of the new-wave country that flooded the online platforms of generation Z.

He rightly suspected that his cousin had probably made a handsome fee for his efforts in setting up this impromptu performance, and Ryan would see to it that Felix never worked in the music industry again.

But, for that night, Ryan had decided, the show had to go on. Priding himself as the consummate professional that he was, he would get this gig over and done with as fast as possible (and get back to a place where there was a *Pret A Manger* on every corner).

As he prepared to tune his guitar, the young country singer heard a *knock* on his dressing room door (if a person could actually call this former storeroom a dressing room in the first place).

"Come in," he called.

The door swung open and in walked Sandy with a tray of sandwiches and a mug of tea. "Sorry to interrupt," said the local café worker. "I'm here on behalf of our catering team." She let out an embarrassed grin. "Well, technically, I *am* the catering team. My boss was supposed to help out, but he's already started on the *Stellas*."

Ryan refused to give her eye contact and waited for the tray to be placed down in front of him.

"There's tuna, egg, cheese and ham." Sandy pointed at each pile with a proud expression. "We like to give our talent a wide choice, you see. People always have various dietary requirements."

The young man stared at her. "I'm vegan."

"Oh, splendid! That's a good job I made the egg ones, then. You'll find some cress in there, too, you lucky veggie." Sandy placed down the mug of tea. "Now, I hope you like your tea strong. Before I go —" She reached across and began rummaging through his drawer. Ryan watched in disbelief as she pulled out a set of keys. "Don't mind me! Just need to get access to the cleaning cupboard. There's been a terrible mess in the men's toilets tonight. I'd only go if you have to."

Sandy gave him a farewell wave and hurried out of the room. Once she was back out into the hallway, she closed Ryan's dressing room door and locked it with her set of keys. The echoes of Ryan's furious cries followed her all the way to the other end of the corridor, where her boss, Hywel, was eagerly waiting for her.

"Here," she said, handing over the keys with a disapproving shake of her head. "The things I do for you."

Hywel let out a sly grin. "Did you give the man his tea?"

Sandy saw the look on his face, and her eyes widened. "What did you put in there?"

"Oh, just a little something to give him a good night. He'll need it being locked in a broom cupboard for a few hours. Hope he's not too much of a lightweight."

"You wicked man!"

The café owner chuckled and made his way back into the main hall. Julie and Simon, Barmouth's resident country duo, were in the middle of their rendition of "It Ain't Me, Babe", whilst the encouraging audience clapped along.

Hywel weaved his way through the crowd and headed towards the small bar at the back of the hall. Noel was waiting for him, and gave the man a knowing nod as he approached.

"Is our friend taken care of?" Noel asked.

Hywel scratched his giant sideburns and nodded. "Don't you worry about Ed Sheeran. He's not playing anything tonight."

Noel slipped him a twenty-pound note. "Glad to hear it. Get yourself a drink."

Over on the other side of the hall, Nesta and Darren were standing amongst the large group of country enthusiasts, sipping on their soft drinks, as the current act continued their performance.

"You really think he didn't do it?" Darren asked with another gulp of warm cola.

Nesta shook her head. She thought about their conversation with Gethin Moore in the yard and how tragic the outcome had been. "Gethin Moore is a lot of things, but he's not a killer."

"How can you be so sure?"

"If there's one thing I'm quite certain about in an investigation like this — it's that you can never be sure." Darren let her words sink in but was none the wiser. "Without a time machine," Nesta continued, "nobody can ever be a hundred percent certain of how a person died unless they were there. Even when a killer is arrested with an insurmountable amount of evidence, the police are still at the mercy of a judge and jury. It's not like these detective programmes where the sleuth solves the case as though it were fact and that's the end of the whole thing. There's a whole trial that goes on afterwards. It's all an educated guess based on the facts."

Darren was now even more confused. "So what's the point, then? Surely people want to know who actually did it."

"We're just like that man on the bridge," said Nesta. "We're just fishing. Our job is to gather as many facts as possible. Then, it's up to the person that receives them to make their own judgement. In our case, it's the viewers on the internet. But, most importantly, there's one person's judgement I care the most about."

"And who's that?" asked Darren.

Nesta smiled. "Mine," she said. "And based on everything I've seen so far, Gethin Moore is not our killer." She gazed around at the crowd of locals. "The jury is very much still out on this one."

They both began scanning the room. There were plenty of familiar faces around that night: Noel and his group of merry musicians; Nia Llywelyn. the festival director; Robin Lock, the bruised talent manager; Hywel and Sandy from the café; Anwen and Richard Neville; Nick Franklin with his broken foot; Susan Tapscott, the gallery owner, and, finally — Kenny Leith.

Nesta almost did a double-take and watched the videographer filming away with his phone. She swallowed the rest of her drink and went marching towards him. "*You!*"

Kenny took one look at the determined woman coming towards him and made a quick dash for the nearest side door.

"Ladies and gentleman!" cried a voice from the stage. "It's time to welcome our next act for the evening." Nia Llywelyn stood behind the microphone with a beaming grin. "Give it up for The Golden Wanderers!"

The room erupted into applause, as Noel and his band began setting up. To Nesta and Darren's surprise, Nick Franklin was carried up onto stage by two local men and plonked into the drummer's stool.

"We have a new drummer tonight," said Noel, re-adjusting his microphone. "Luckily, he only needs the one foot!"

The audience laughed, and a furious Susan Tapscott finished her drink and stormed out of the room.

Nick Franklin, who hadn't played the drums for many years, looked very pleased with himself and raised his drumsticks like a returning hero. Nesta and Darren both smiled.

The main doors flung open, and a bald man with an expensive coat and a gold chain stepped into the room.

Nesta saw the excited look on Robin Lock's face and leant over to mutter in Darren's ear. "That must be the record label man."

Darren took one look at the pair of Aviator sunglasses across the man's eyes and watched him strutting to the bar in search of a cocktail. "You don't say..."

The Golden Wanderers launched into their opening song, and the audience began bobbing their heads in time with the music. Nesta tapped her foot and turned to her disinterested friend. "They're not bad."

A proud Robin began taking frequent glances towards Cliff Booth, the owner of *Rooftop Records*. He hoped that his new and improved group was making an impression, although Cliff showed little emotion.

As the song went on, Noel appeared to be getting more and more agitated. "Keep in time," he hissed towards his drummer. "Keep in time, you idiot!"

Nick, who was doing his best considering that he was a last-minute replacement, gave him a helpless shrug.

Even Nesta had started to notice the drumming was severely lagging.

"I think they need another drummer," Darren muttered, wincing at the messy performance.

Robin had started to become nervous and could see his front man's blood pressure rising all the way from the back of the auditorium. "Speed up, speed up..."

Nick's confidence only got worse, and he began to sweat as they reached the chorus.

Noel could see Cliff Booth checking his watch, and the front man turned around to face his drummer. "If you don't keep up, I'm going to come back there and hit you with that crash cymbal!"

A furious Nick gave the front man a rude hand gesture and chucked his drum sticks.

Noel wailed as one of the drum sticks struck him in the back of the head. Before he could realise what had just happened, the stage was invaded by a furious Ryan Kirby.

The audience gasped, as the young singer began assaulting the band's equipment like a delirious member of The Who.

A surprised Hywel turned to Sandy, who was clasping her mouth in shock. "How the devil did he get loose?"

His café worker shrugged, and they both turned back to witness the carnage.

Robin Lock clutched his own face in sheer despair, having seen that the unimpressed Cliff had already left.

Ryan Kirby pushed Noel out of the way and grabbed the microphone. It soon became clear that the young man was incredibly intoxicated, and he began rambling about never coming back to the festival ever again.

After a chorus of loud booing from the audience, Nesta looked around in search of a person she hadn't seen since they arrived.

Kenny Leith was sitting within the safe confinements of the men's toilet cubicles. The man was pouring over his recent footage like a euphoric child at Halloween, until he heard a loud knock on his cubicle door.

"I know you're in there!" a woman's voice cried. Kenny cowered on his toilet seat, as the person continued knocking. "You can't hide from me forever!"

CHAPTER 23

The footage on Kenny Leith's phone had confirmed Nesta's growing suspicions. After all, Kenny still held a glimpse into the last few days of Dale Benham's life, and, from what she had seen, the man's state of mind was anything but stable.

"What do you mean you've already seen it?" Nesta asked, as she drove back across the rickety Penmaenpool toll bridge (in her view, there was no such thing as too many times).

"The guy posted it all online," said Darren, munching on a stick of original Barmouth rock. "I thought I told you."

"You most certainly did not," Nesta snapped, having spent far more time than she had wanted to in a grubby men's bathroom.

"He probably couldn't help himself. The man seems to post everything on that channel. No wonder he's hardly got any views. It's quality over quantity."

Nesta was still cross at having to chase down a man whose hygiene levels were about as high as *The Mountain Theatre*'s male toilets. "Did you see the footage of him talking about Blas Yr Halen?"

"Wasn't that the name of the house we found?"

"Very good," said Nesta. "Sounds like someone's paying attention."

Darren hated it when she spoke to him like a teacher. He looked down to see that the Jack Russell between his feet was gazing up at his stick of rock. "What was all that dark stuff about vengeance and family about?"

Nesta took a right turn onto the A493, a road which would take them past Fairbourne and along a scenic coastal route. Their final destination was a village called Llwyngwril (which had been included in Dale Benham's address book).

"You noticed that, too?" Nesta asked, deliberating the teenager's question.

"Course I did," said Darren. "The guy ranted about it on almost every video."

Nesta nodded. The series of Dale's drunken rants into Kenny Leith's camera phone had indeed consisted of many uses of the words "family" and "vengeance". However, it was hard to know whether the man had been talking about taking revenge *for* his family or *against* them. "I didn't like the way he was talking one bit."

"You think he was serious about the revenge thing?" Darren asked.

"It's hard to know," said Nesta. "People say a lot of stupid things that they don't mean whilst under the influence. But I'm certain of one thing — Dale was more interested in the actual cottage we saw than the person inside it. Did you watch all of the videos?"

Darren scoffed. "Are you kidding? You know how much video content there is out there? I'm not spending all my time watching everything Kenny Leith puts up. The guy's a hack."

"Sounds like you missed the part about the relevance of that cottage," said Nesta. She stared out through her windscreen at the steep, winding road.

Darren was already beginning to feel queasy and had become more focused on his stomach.

"There was this one video where Dale talked about his mother," Nesta continued. "He was less angry in this one and more reflective. He spoke about his mother, Lydia, and how she had grown up in that cottage we saw with her younger sister. It was their childhood home."

"That must have been a very long time ago," said Darren. "The place was falling apart. I don't know how anyone could live there now."

Nesta's gaze remained focused on the road, but her mind was elsewhere. "It clearly meant a lot to Dale and his mother. Which is understandable. Childhood homes hold a lot of memories."

Darren leant forward and picked up Dale's address book from the dashboard. "So why are we going to this Danny's house? Shouldn't we be checking out the old cottage again?"

"Oh, we'll be paying a visit to the cottage. Don't you worry. First, I would like to see if we can find out more about the history of Dale's family." She pointed to the address book. "I'm still hoping that this Danny is a relative."

Nesta's old *Citroën* drove its way south along the coastal road in the direction of Tywyn and Aberdyfi. Darren was just on the verge of begging his driver to pull over, when they came across a sign that read: Llwyngwril. The small village had a population of around six hundred people and included a shop, a local pub and a distinctly blue-coloured chapel. But the most notable features of this quiet village (at least for Nesta) were the vast amount of knitted items dotted around every corner. Known as "The Knitted Village" (and for embracing the phenomenon known as Yarn Bombing), Llwyngwril was a place that took pride in its crochet and knitting needles and had gone to great lengths in stopping traffic with a whole host of elaborate creations (most notably — a red dragon and a man with a giant head that popped over the side of the main bridge).

Darren had to rub his eyes a few times to make sure that he hadn't fallen asleep and pointed to the enormous, woollen head, as they crossed over the stone bridge. "Is that for real?" he asked.

"If by real you mean — is that a real person? Then, no. He's been knitted."

The teenager turned to give his driver a scowl. "I know he's *knitted*. I mean — what have the people of this village been smoking?"

Nesta ignored his question and turned off the main road into a narrow lane. "I think it's all lovely. Imagine living in a village that loves knitting? It's like my dream come true."

Darren had forgotten how much his driver enjoyed knitting. He had even had the pleasure of trying to sell her own various creations on a Mold market stall but was still recovering from that experience. "I just don't get it, that's all."

"What's not to get? Knitting's fun!" Nesta pulled up the hand brake after parking near a narrow foot path. She checked her map again and nodded. "This must be the place."

Her passenger peered out of his window and saw that the lane they were on led to a small house further down. "Are we bringing Hari?" he asked.

"Absolutely," said Nesta. "You can never be too careful in situations like this. We need all the protection we can get."

Darren raised a cynical eyebrow and took another look at their supposed "protection" snoring in the footwell.

The small house at the bottom of the lane seemed like the perfect spot to hide away from the world. Located well off the beaten path in a sleepy village meant that it rarely received visitors, and now it had three: Nesta, Darren and Hari entered through its front gate and made the short walk to the front door.

The condition of the front garden was a stark contrast to the one they had seen via the drone, and it appeared that its owner took pride in having it well-maintained.

When Danny Cecil opened up his front door, he had to re-adjust his glasses. "Oh," he said. "I'm sorry. I thought you were the postman."

Nesta gave him a friendly smile. "We're not delivering parcels today, I'm afraid."

Danny appeared to have a rather shy and gentle demeanour, and the middle-aged man did not seem to be in the mood for a social visit. With a name like Danny, Nesta had imagined meeting a more lively individual — like the type of person who could take a quick look under a stranger's car bonnet. Instead, she was met with someone who seemed more confident with an upcoming tax return. It all went to show, she realised, that you couldn't judge a person by their name (and that she had to stop falling for such silly stereotypes).

"Can I help you?" Danny asked.

"Yes," said Nesta. "I'm quite certain you can."

Ten minutes later, and Danny found himself boiling the kettle for guests he had not even asked for. Somehow, unbe-knownst to himself, this peculiar woman from out of town (or village in the case of Llwyngwril) had managed to convince him that it would be a great idea to have a round of teas and a plate of biscuits. He had to be much stronger next time, Danny thought to himself, or he would end up with a horde of sales-people in his front room.

"How do you know Dale again?" he asked whilst opening up the cupboard in search of a biscuit tin.

"It's complicated," said Nesta, who was struck by the amount of musical equipment in his kitchen. "But I believe you and Dale know each other?"

Danny turned around with a confused face. "Of course. He's my cousin."

Nesta felt a surge of relief throughout her body. The trip to Llwyngwril had been worth it after all (and not just for the knitted items). "First cousin?"

"Our mothers were sisters," said Danny.

"Interesting," said Nesta. "I've heard all about your aunt. She moved to Texas and married a wealthy oil tycoon."

There was a loud *bang*, as Darren accidentally bashed the guitar in his hands. He had located the instrument on the other side of the room and looked back at the other two with a sheepish face. "Sorry about that. Just checking out the six string."

Nesta threw him a furious stare for interrupting, and she cringed as the teenager began playing the opening bars to his new song, "Jolene". "You seem very musical like your cousin," she said eventually.

Danny let out a nervous laugh. "I wouldn't go that far. Dale was a much better guitar player than I am." He pointed to the electronic keyboard overlooking the window. "I'm okay on the piano. But I wouldn't say I'm much of a musician."

Nesta looked over at the piles of sheet music everywhere, some of which were printed and the rest drawn out in pencil. "You could have fooled me. If you're not a musician with all this stuff lying around, then Elton John is a plummer."

Her compliment caused the man to lower his guard, and he gave her an appreciative smile. "You could say I'm more of a songwriter. Well, technically, I suppose I *am* a songwriter. Just not a wealthy one."

"A very modest songwriter," said Nesta with a suspicious stare. "You write songs for a living?"

Danny placed the teas down on the kitchen table and took a seat. "I used to. I suppose I'm more of a composer these days. I put together scores for television programmes and adverts. Nothing groundbreaking."

Nesta continued her long stare. "Tell me," she said. "Did you by any chance write Dale's songs?"

The man was shocked by her unexpected question. "Whatever makes you ask that question? Dale writes all of his own songs."

"Goodness," said Nesta. "You're a modest man, Danny, but you're a terrible liar."

Danny's face went bright red. "Uh, I don't know what you mean?"

"I admire your willingness to maintain your cousin's musical legacy even after his death. It can't have been easy not getting any of the credit all these years."

The man sighed. She was right — he really *was* a terrible liar. "It wasn't that hard. I just love the process."

"Of writing songs?"

Danny nodded. "I've been doing it all my life. I don't care who sings them or who people *think* wrote them. That's not where the buzz comes from." He looked over at the guitar on Darren's lap whilst the Dolly Parton song continued in the background. "It's hearing your song played for the first time by a talented artist. And that's what Dale was. He may not have written his own music, but he could play like nobody else."

Nesta looked around his kitchen at the musical memorabilia lying around the room. "So there was Lydia and your mother. Just the two sisters?"

"Catrin," said Danny. "Her name was Catrin."

"Catrin..." Nesta gathered from his use of the past tense that Catrin was no longer around. "Did Dale have any brothers or sisters?"

Danny shook his head. "He was an only child. I've got one sibling who still lives in the area."

"And who owns Blas Yr Halen?"

The mention of the cottage that his mother grew up in made the man uncomfortable. "Uh, well, that's —"

"Complicated?"

There was a long pause, and Nesta was forced to listen to another few bars of Darren's song again.

"Lydia had bought the property outright after my grand-mother died." Danny began scratching his finger nails against the wood on his kitchen table. "She could afford to do that, obvi-ously, with her great wealth."

"But she didn't move back to live in it?"

Danny scoffed. "Lydia? She had no intention of returning to Barmouth. There's a reason she moved away in the first place. She had this idea in her head that she was better than everyone. So, she just bought her childhood home and let it rot away for years."

"That must have been hard for your mother," said Nesta.

"It was hard for all of us in the family." His eyes had become red with anger. "There was nothing my mother could do about it. She didn't have any money. The woman had to work for everything she had, and she never had a penny to her name, even until the day she died. All whilst her sister was living it up in some ranch over in America. But we had everything we needed growing up. Her children didn't know any different. She put food on the table, and we had a happy childhood." His mood lifted. "My mother really loved her musicals, you see. She'd find ways to sneak us into shows and film screenings. It wasn't until later that I discovered how miserable her life was during those years."

Nesta listened with a growing concern. "How old are you Danny?"

"Forty-five."

"And you're the eldest?"

The man nodded.

"I believe Dale was in his early sixties, wasn't he?" Nesta was busy running some numbers in her head.

"There was a large gap between Lydia and my mother," said Danny.

"Yes," said Nesta. "There must have been." Her little theory would have to wait for now, and she decided to ask the man a question that had been plaguing her all day: "Can I ask you something, Danny? Who did your Aunt Lydia leave her childhood home to when she died?"

Danny didn't even need to think about the answer. "The same person living there now."

CHAPTER 24

The rest of the conversation with Danny had involved a lot more questions. Suddenly, the last known footage of Dale Benham was starting to make more sense. The constant mention of "family" and "betrayal" had been far more than just a drunken rant, and Nesta feared that there had been another life at stake.

Dale had always confided in his cousin, Danny, both musically and on a personal level. His final visit before he died had been a tense and uncomfortable one.

The drive back from Llwyngwril had been mostly silent, as Nesta tried to process everything that she had heard.

"Do we really have to go straight there now?" Darren asked, as they drove in the direction of Blas Yr Halen.

"We need to be certain," said Nesta.

Darren sighed. Little did the teenager know it then, but he was soon about to come face to face with Dale Benham's killer.

THE CONDITION of Blas Yr Halen was as bad as it had appeared on the drone footage. Nesta, Darren and Hari had to wade through a long series of overgrown stinging nettles just to get to the front door. After a solid *knock*, they waited for a response. It was hard to believe that this rundown property was once the happy childhood home of Lydia Benham, and Nesta tried to picture two young girls playing in the front garden.

"Don't think anyone's home," said Darren, who was keen to get some lunch in his stomach.

As Nesta was about to agree, the front door slid open to reveal a familiar face. The current owner of Blas Yr Halen stared at the people on her doorstep with a worried face.

"What are you guys doing here?"

"Sandy," said Nesta. "I was beginning to think you might be at the café."

The woman smiled. "Hywel's a right slavedriver, but he does give me some days off. And that's only because he's closed today."

Nesta felt an uneasiness in her stomach. "Do you mind if we come in?"

Sandy was used to serving teas and coffees but never in her own home.

"Sorry about the state of this place," she said, leading her guests through the hallway and into the kitchen. "It's definitely a fixer upper, and I've got a lot of jobs to get through. But renovation costs are not cheap."

There was a smell of dampness in the air from years of neglect. Mould covered the walls and ceilings, and the floorboards wobbled underfoot.

"It has lots of potential," said Nesta, taking her seat at a fold-up table. "It can't be easy on your own."

Darren remained standing with Hari and paced around in a

sulk. He had no intention of drinking anymore tea that day and felt that their visit to Llwyngwril had been long enough.

"I quite like being on my own," said Sandy, boiling her kettle on an old AGA oven. "I've had a few relationships over the years. Sometimes I think having another person in your life is more hassle than it's worth."

Nesta could see Darren giving her an impatient look and decided to cut to the chase. "We've just been speaking with your brother."

Sandy's posture tightened. "Danny?"

"I was trying to work out the numbers," said Nesta. "You mentioned that your mother was a big *Grease* fan. That film would have come out a couple of years before your brother was born. Danny and Sandy — she really *did* love that film."

Sandy smiled at the thought of her mother. "She was quite a character, my mam."

"A hard-working woman, too, from what I heard." Nesta saw that the woman was uncomfortable. "You never told us that Dale was your cousin."

Sandy laughed. "It's not something I shout from the rooftops about every time I get a new customer. Besides, Dale and I didn't really get on."

"I suspected that," said Nesta. "In fact, your brother mentioned that Dale made some pretty strong accusations when he last saw him. It was shortly before he died."

Sandy's hands began to shake, and she almost dropped the mug in her hand. "What kind of accusations?"

Nesta tried to find the best way to word what she was about to say, but, ultimately, there was no sugarcoating it. "He said you killed his mother."

The woman at the stove glared at her. "That's rich coming from him," she snapped.

"Why do you say that?"

"Because he tried to murder me in my sleep!" Sandy cried. There was a long silence, and she covered her mouth as though the words had forced their way out. She could feel her heart racing, as the horrors of that night came flooding back in the form of adrenaline. "I'm sorry," she said. "I didn't mean to — I still haven't quite recovered."

Nesta stood up and headed over to the AGA. She placed a hand on the woman's shoulder. "It's alright," she said. "Just breathe."

Sandy nodded and closed her eyes before Nesta walked her over to the nearest chair. "I never meant for any of this to happen the way it did." Tears began streaming down her face like a burden had suddenly been lifted.

"Why don't you start from the beginning," said Nesta, insisting on finishing off the teas herself.

"A few years before Auntie Lydia died," said Sandy, "I went over to stay with her in Texas. It was the first time I'd been abroad. Whilst I was out there, she offered me a job. Their house was enormous, and they had acres of land. Her health was already deteriorating, and I'd trained as a nurse. I became her live-in carer. All her medications, meals, everything — it was all done through me. We got to know each other very well."

Nesta handed her a mug of tea. "I heard she suffered from dementia."

Sandy nodded. "It got really bad by the end. It was sad to see as we'd really bonded. I think she saw my mam in me, and she missed her sister a lot. Mam would never believe that, but it's all Lydia talked about towards the end. She also missed Barmouth, and I'd tell her what had changed — and what *hadn't* changed."

"Dale was also close with his mother, wasn't he?"

The question made Sandy cringe. "Their relationship was

always strange. He acted like he was a great son, but he was very controlling. I think he became jealous of how close I'd become with Lydia and even tried to sack me. But Lydia wouldn't allow it. As she deteriorated, Dale started blaming me."

"She blamed you for his mother's health?" Nesta asked.

"He was very paranoid and suspicious. His mother was very wealthy and people had tried to take advantage of that before — or, at least, that's what he said. Dale barely had any money at that stage of his career. Lydia used to say he was terrible with his finances and should have lived beneath his means during the more successful years of his career."

Nesta thought about the man's cheap lifestyle, living in free accommodation and campervans. "It sounds like he was waiting for some inheritance to come through."

Sandy laughed. "You can say that again. I would have loved to see his face when he found out that almost all of his mother's fortune had been left to charity. I think it was Lydia's way of teaching her son an important lesson in financial planning."

"And this place?" Nesta looked around the kitchen. "She left this house to you?"

"I couldn't believe it." Sandy nodded and nursed her tea. "I don't know if it was the dementia talking, but Lydia had begun to regret leaving this place unoccupied for all these years. Her own sister had not been able to afford her own home, and Lydia had originally bought the place out of spite when the two had fallen out. Leaving the house to me was her strange way of making amends."

"But that's not how Dale saw it?"

Sandy shuddered. "He was furious. The man thought that I'd slowly poisoned her — that I'd coerced his mother into writing me into her will. But he could never prove it. Dale had always loved Barmouth. I think he'd hoped to have this house for himself." She took a deep breath. "The guy had always been a little unhinged. Danny didn't believe me, but I knew Dale had a violent streak in him. His mother's death brought out his true colours in the end. He began stalking me to start with."

"Dale was stalking *you*?"

"He used to turn up everywhere — at the café, at the shops, on my own doorstep... To begin with, he was just trying to make me nervous. And it worked really well. Then I started getting these letters... they were signed by Lydia, as if she was writing from beyond the grave, threatening me. I knew it had to be him, but it didn't stop me freaking out and getting paranoid. The letters said that she knew who killed her. Later, they became death threats." Tears began to reform in her wide eyes. "I remember waking up in the middle of the night. And he was standing there like a ghost."

Nesta didn't even need to ask who she was referring to this time.

"Dale was towering over me," Sandy continued. "It's like he was dead behind the eyes. I couldn't see it at first, but he was holding this wire in his hands." She cleared her throat. "Then, he began choking me. He kept shouting 'you killed her!', but I couldn't even shout back." She took a hard gulp and became angry. "On the bedside table, there was this sculpture I'd picked up in America. It was shaped like an owl, and it was really solid and heavy enough to use like a dumbbell. He was still choking me, and I grabbed the object and whacked it against the side of his head. The wire around my neck loosened straight away, and Dale flopped to the floor. I thought I'd killed him then and there. I ran out of the room and locked myself in the bathroom. I kept picturing his body, lying there on the bedroom floor. I'd hit his head really hard, and there was still some blood on my hand. After about ten minutes, I just needed to get out of that house. I snuck out of the bathroom and headed straight outside into the front garden." Her face went pale. "That's when I saw him again."

"Dale was outside?" Nesta asked.

Sandy nodded. "He was cycling off in the distance. I couldn't believe it. He didn't look very steady, but there he was, still alive. I couldn't go back inside the house, so I jumped straight in the car and headed to my brother's. The next day, we both heard that Dale's body had been found on the bridge."

Nesta nodded. "He must have been trying to get back to his guesthouse. They found his bike in a ditch nearby. You said he looked unsteady. He must have fallen off his bike and decided to walk the rest of the way. That head injury really was fatal after all."

The woman opposite her was now numb. "A part of me was relieved that he was finally dead. I'd never have to worry about him again. Then came the realisation that I'd killed him. Danny said it was foolish to go to the police. People go to prison for assaulting burglars — let alone killing them. The whole self-defence argument is pointless. So we decided not to tell anyone."

Nesta could see the inner turmoil in the woman's face. "And how has that been working out for you?"

Sandy lowered her head. "Honestly? It's been hell."

Nesta and Darren both looked at each other. When they headed back outside to the welcome breeze of fresh air, there wasn't much more to be said. Still, Darren had one question that was playing on his mind, and he waited until they were back inside the car until he asked it: "Do you think she *did* actually kill Dale's mother?"

Nesta placed her hands on the steering wheel and thought about the woman they had just left in tears. "It's like I said before," she said, firing up the engine. "You can never be certain with anything."

Darren nodded and began searching around for his half-eaten stick of rock. He looked up into the rear view mirror and saw a smug Hari standing on the back seat with a colourful stick in his mouth. "Hey!!"

CHAPTER 25

Richard Neville could have sworn he had heard something buzzing. If what he could hear was indeed a wasp or a bee, then he had a serious problem on his hands.

The man stopped digging for a moment and wiped the sweat from his forehead. It was a productive afternoon, so far, and he had reached the end of his little project. Disposing the remains of such a sensitive matter was not easy in broad daylight, and, in another ten minutes, he would be rid of his problem forever. He had initially considered a bonfire before deciding that the far corners of his back garden were safe enough. Nobody ever ventured down there, and his wife had little interest in gardening.

As he turned back to his wheelbarrow, Richard caught sight of something hovering above his head. It certainly wasn't a bird or an insect and was now low enough for him to swipe at with his shovel.

"Get away!" he roared, waving his tool around in the air.

The drone began toying with him and moved in and out of range.

Over in the guesthouse, Darren was sitting on his bed chuckling. He fiddled with the remote control in his hand and saw Richard Neville's furious face on his monitor. His last night at Bryn Lodge had been a much more relaxing experience now that he was able to rule out Anwen Neville as Dale's killer. But there was still the matter of the mysterious burials in their back garden, and he had been determined to discover the truth before he left.

As he caught a glimpse of what exactly Richard had been trying to hide in that back garden, he heard a chilling scream.

Darren leapt off the bed and came running out into the hallway. Nesta had also bolted out of her room and was focusing her attention on a distraught Anwen.

Her guests hurried to join her over at the doorway of Dale Benham's old room and were equally surprised to discover that his possessions had vanished.

"It's all gone!" Anwen cried. "All of it!" She pointed at the bare room. "First, it was my records, now, everything relating to that man has disappeared. It's all been stolen!"

The woman began sobbing, until she noticed an amused Darren beside her. "You!" she roared. "It was you! I should have known it!"

"Now," said Nesta. "Darren couldn't have possibly —" She paused and grew suspicious of the teenager's big smile. "Did you?"

Darren lifted up the monitor to his drone and showed it to Anwen. "I think you'd better speak with your husband. He's in the back garden."

A horrified Anwen stormed off back to her house. Nesta and Darren followed her all the way to the back garden and saw a guilty-looking Richard Neville standing by his flower bed.

"What on earth do you think you're doing?!" Anwen took

one look at her favourite singer's belongings, which were now dumped in a rusty wheelbarrow, and wailed.

Realising that the game was up, Richard threw down his shovel and prepared to defend his actions. "What does it look like I'm doing? Do you know how sick and tired I am of hearing that man's music all day every day? Ever since we met, it's been Dale this and Dale that — then we have him under our roof. Finally, I'm rid of the man, and now I have to see all his stuff everywhere! This is my house, too!"

Anwen shook her head in disgust. "You really are a sick man."

"*I'm* the sick one?! I'm not the one who built a shrine for some idiot in a cowboy hat!"

The argument continued, until Anwen grabbed the shovel and began chasing her husband around the garden.

Nesta and Darren couldn't help but smile, as they saw a vinyl record poking up from the hole in Richard's flower bed. The cover photo of Dale Benham was sticking out from the dirt, his face staring back at them with that dashing smile.

JOIN THE P. L. HANDLEY NEWSLETTER

If you would like to be the first to receive the latest updates on the next Nesta Griffiths book, make sure to join the P. L. Handley newsletter by going to the P. L. Handley website.

www.plhandley.com

Whilst you're waiting for Book 6 in the Nesta Griffiths Mysteries, why not try the first book in another P. L Handley murder mystery series:

The Murder Ledger

Available on Amazon

THE MURDER LEDGER

When an elderly lottery winner goes missing in a small, rural town, it's up to a tenacious, local reporter to solve the case. Aided by a curious accountant with a methodical brain, Rhiannon must use her new (and unlikely) partnership to uncover a series of shocking secrets.

www.plhandley.com

ALSO BY P. L. HANDLEY

The Body At Bala Lake

The Murder At Talacre Beach

The Mystery At Mold Market

The Corpse In A Chester Hotel

Death On Barmouth Bridge

The Murder Ledger

Death By Numbers

The Final Score

The Penny Mystery

The Bottom Line

The Broken Heart

The Wrong Turn

REVIEWS

We hope you enjoyed this book. Reviews are extremely important for new authors, so please do feel free to write a short review on the book's Amazon page. It will be an enormous help in introducing this series to new readers.

THANK YOU FOR READING

www.plhandley.com